Praise for the #1 New York Times
bestselling In Death series

"Sexy, gritty, richly imagined suspense."
—*Publishers Weekly*

"Groundbreaking."   —*The Romance Reader*

"Another taut, gut-wrenching, compelling thriller from the incomparable J.D. Robb (Nora Roberts). Each new installment in this series adds more layers to already complex, fascinating characters. And the storylines are always first-rate. Need I say more—another masterpiece!"
—*ParaNormal Romance Reviews*

"Tough-talking thriller with a matchless pace."
—*Kirkus Reviews*

"A well-written, action-packed book that has surprises in it that keep you enthralled till the last sentence of the last page . . . Watching the characters and their rapport develop has been delightful to behold. Ms. Robb has yet again shown what a great suspense author she is. Well done!"
—*The Romance Readers Connection*

"Fast-paced romantic suspense."   —*The Best Reviews*

"A unique blend of hard-core police drama, science fiction and passionate romance."   —*Gothic Journal*

"Fantastic."   —*The Paperback Forum*

MIDNIGHT IN DEATH

J. D. Robb

BERKLEY BOOKS, NEW YORK

THE BERKLEY PUBLISHING GROUP
Published by the Penguin Group
Penguin Group (USA) Inc.
375 Hudson Street, New York, New York 10014, USA
Penguin Group (Canada), 90 Eglinton Avenue East, Suite 700, Toronto, Ontario M4P 2Y3, Canada
(a division of Pearson Penguin Canada Inc.)
Penguin Books Ltd., 80 Strand, London WC2R 0RL, England
Penguin Group Ireland, 25 St. Stephen's Green, Dublin 2, Ireland (a division of Penguin Books Ltd.)
Penguin Group (Australia), 250 Camberwell Road, Camberwell, Victoria 3124, Australia
(a division of Pearson Australia Group Pty. Ltd.)
Penguin Books India Pvt. Ltd., 11 Community Centre, Panchsheel Park, New Delhi—110 017, India
Penguin Group (NZ), Cnr. Airborne and Rosedale Roads, Albany, Auckland 1310, New Zealand
(a division of Pearson New Zealand Ltd.)
Penguin Books (South Africa) (Pty.) Ltd., 24 Sturdee Avenue, Rosebank, Johannesburg 2196,
South Africa

Penguin Books Ltd., Registered Offices: 80 Strand, London WC2R 0RL, England

Previously published in the anthology *Silent Night*, published by Jove Publications, Inc.

This is a work of fiction. Names, characters, places, and incidents either are the product of the author's imagination or are used fictitiously, and any resemblance to actual persons, living or dead, business establishments, events, or locales is entirely coincidental. The publisher does not have any control over and does not assume any responsibility for author or third-party websites or their content.

MIDNIGHT IN DEATH

A Berkley Book / published by arrangement with the author

PRINTING HISTORY
Berkley edition / October 2005

Copyright © 1998 by Nora Roberts.

ISBN: 0-425-20881-8

BERKLEY®
Berkley Books are published by The Berkley Publishing Group,
a division of Penguin Group (USA) Inc.,
375 Hudson Street, New York, New York 10014.
BERKLEY is a registered trademark of Penguin Group (USA) Inc.
The "B" design is a trademark belonging to Penguin Group (USA) Inc.

PRINTED IN THE UNITED STATES OF AMERICA

10 9 8 7 6 5 4 3 2 1

The year is dying in the night.

—TENNYSON

The welfare of the people is the chief law.

—CICERO

ONE

Murder respects no traditions. It ignores sentiment. It takes no holidays.

Because murder was her business, Lieutenant Eve Dallas stood in the predawn freeze of Christmas morning coating the deerskin gloves her husband had given her only hours before with Seal-It.

The call had come in less than an hour before and less than six hours since she'd closed a case that had left her shaky and exhausted. Her first Christmas with Roarke wasn't getting off to a rousing start.

Then again, it had taken a much nastier turn for Judge Harold Wainger.

His body had been dumped dead center in the ice rink at Rockefeller Center. Face up, so his glazed eyes could stare at the huge celebrational tree that was New York's symbol of goodwill toward men.

His body was naked and already a deep shade of blue. The thick mane of silver hair that had been his trademark had been roughly chopped off. And though his face was severely battered, she had no trouble recognizing him.

She'd sat in his courtroom dozens of times in her ten years on the force. He had been, she thought, a solid and steady man, with as much understanding of the slippery channels of the law as respect for the heart of it.

She crouched down to get a closer look at the words that had been burned deeply into his chest.

JUDGE NOT, LEST YOU BE JUDGED

She hoped the burns had been inflicted postmortem, but she doubted it.

He had been mercilessly beaten, the fingers of both hands broken. Deep wounds around his wrists and ankles indicated that he'd been bound. But it hadn't been the beating or the burns that killed him.

The rope used to hang him was still around his neck, digging deep into flesh. Even that wouldn't have been quick, she decided. It didn't appear that his neck had been broken, and the burst vessels in his eyes and face signaled slow strangulation.

"He wanted you alive as long as possible," she murmured. "He wanted you to feel it all."

Kneeling now, she studied the handwritten note that was flapping gaily in the wind. It had been fixed over the judge's groin like an obscene loincloth. The list of names had been printed in careful square block letters.

JUDGE HAROLD WAINGER
PROSECUTING ATTORNEY STEPHANIE RING
PUBLIC DEFENDER CARL NEISSAN
JUSTINE POLINSKY
DOCTOR CHARLOTTE MIRA
LIEUTENANT EVE DALLAS

"Saving me for last, Dave?"

She recognized the style: gleeful infliction of pain followed by a slow, torturous death. David Palmer enjoyed his work. His experiments, as he'd called them when Eve had finally hunted him down three years before.

By the time she'd gotten him into a cage, he had eight victims to his credit, and with them an extensive file of discs recording his work. Since then he'd been serving the eight life-term sentences that Wainger had given him in a maximum-security ward for mental defectives.

"But you got out, didn't you, Dave? This is your handiwork. The torture, the humiliations, the burns. Public dumping spot for the body. No copycat here. Bag him," she ordered and got wearily to her feet.

It didn't look as though the last days of December 2058 were going to be much of a party.

The minute she was back in her vehicle, Eve ordered the heat on full blast. She stripped off her gloves and rubbed her hands over her face. She would have to go in and file her report, but the first order of business couldn't wait for her to drive to her home office. Damn if she was going to spend Christmas Day at Cop Central.

She used the in-dash 'link to contact Dispatch and arrange to have each name on the list notified of possible jeopardy. Christmas or not, she was ordering uniformed guards on each one.

As she drove, she engaged her computer. "Computer, status on David Palmer, mental-defective inmate on Rexal penal facility."

Working. . . . David Palmer, sentenced to eight consecutive life terms in off-planet facility Rexal reported escaped during transport to prison infirmary, December nineteen. Man-hunt ongoing.

"I guess Dave decided to come home for the holidays." She glanced up, scowling, as a blimp cruised over, blasting Christmas tunes as dawn broke over the city. Screw the herald angels, she thought, and called her commander.

"Sir," she said when Whitney's face filled her screen. "I'm sorry to disturb your Christmas."

"I've already been notified about Judge Wainger. He was a good man."

"Yes, sir, he was." She noted that Whitney was wearing a robe—a thick, rich burgundy that she imagined had been a gift from his wife. Roarke was always giving her fancy presents. She wondered if Whitney was as baffled by them as she usually was. "His body's being transferred to the morgue. I have the evidence sealed and am en route to my home office now."

"I would have preferred another primary on this, Lieutenant." He saw her tired eyes flash, the golden brown darkening. Still, her face, with its sharp angles, the firm chin with its shallow dent, the full, unsmiling mouth, stayed cool and controlled.

"Do you intend to remove me from the case?"

"You've just come off a difficult and demanding investigation. Your aide was attacked."

"I'm not calling Peabody in," Eve said quickly. "She's had enough."

"And you haven't?"

She opened her mouth, closed it again. Tricky ground, she acknowledged. "Commander, my name's on the list."

"Exactly. One more reason for you to take a pass here."

Part of her wanted to—the part that wanted, badly, to put it all aside for the day, to go home and have the kind of normal Christmas she'd never experienced. But she thought of Wainger, stripped of all life and all dignity.

"I tracked David Palmer, and I broke him. He was my collar, and no one knows the inside of his mind the way I do."

"Palmer?" Whitney's wide brow furrowed. "Palmer's in prison."

"Not anymore. He escaped on the nineteenth. And he's back, Commander. You could say I recognized his signature. The names on the list," she continued, pressing her point. "They're all connected to him. Wainger was the judge during his trial. Stephanie Ring was APA. Cicely Towers prosecuted the case, but she's dead. Ring assisted. Carl Neissan was his court-appointed attorney when Palmer refused to hire his own counsel, Justine Polinksy served as jury foreman. Dr. Mira tested him and testified against him at trial. I brought him in."

"The names on the list need to be notified."

"Already done, sir, and bodyguards assigned. I can pull

the data from the files into my home unit to refresh my memory, but it's fairly fresh as it is. You don't forget some-one like David Palmer. Another primary will have to start at the beginning, taking time that we don't have. I know this man, how he works, how he thinks. What he wants."

"What he wants, Lieutenant?"

"What he always wanted. Acknowledgment for his ge-nius."

"It's your case, Dallas," Whitney said after a long si-lence. "Close it."

"Yes, sir."

She broke transmission as she drove through the gates of the staggering estate that Roarke had made his home.

Ice from the previous night's storm glinted like silver silk on naked branches. Ornamental shrubs and evergreens glistened with it. Beyond them, the house rose and spread, an elegant fortress, a testament to an earlier century with its beautiful stone, its acres of glass.

In the gloomy half-light of morning, gorgeously deco-rated trees shimmered in several windows. Roarke, she thought with a little smile, had gotten heavily into the Christmas spirit.

Neither of them had had much in the way of pretty hol-iday trees with gaily wrapped gifts stacked under them in their lives. Their childhoods had been miseries, and they had compensated for it in different ways. His had been to acquire, to become one of the richest and most powerful men in the world. By whatever means available. Hers had been to take control, to become part of the system that had failed her when she was a child.

Hers was law. His was—or had been—circumventing law.

Now, not quite a year since another murder had put them on the same ground, they were a unit. She wondered if she would ever understand how they'd managed it.

She left her car out front, walked up the steps and through the door into the kind of wealth that fantasies were made of. Old polished wood, sparkling crystal, ancient rugs lovingly preserved, art that museums would have wept for.

She shrugged off her jacket, started to toss it over the newel post. Then, gritting her teeth, she backtracked and hung it up. She and Summerset, Roarke's aide-de-camp, had declared a tacit truce in their sniping war. There would be no potshots on Christmas, she decided.

She could stand it if he could.

Only marginally pleased that he didn't slither into the foyer and hiss at her as he normally did, Eve headed into the main parlor.

Roarke was there, sitting by the fire, reading the first-edition copy of Yeats that she'd given him. It had been the only gift she'd been able to come up with for the man who not only had everything but owned most of the plants where it was manufactured.

He glanced up, smiled at her. Her stomach fluttered, as it so often did. Just a look, just a smile, and her system went jittery. He looked so . . . perfect, she thought. He was dressed casually for the day, in black, his long, lean body relaxing in a chair probably made two hundred years before.

He had the face of a god with slightly wicked intentions, eyes of blazing Irish blue and a mouth created to destroy a woman's control. Power sat attractively on him, as sleek and sexy, Eve thought, as the rich fall of black hair that skimmed nearly to his shoulders.

He closed the book, set it aside, then held out a hand to her.

"I'm sorry I had to leave." She crossed to him, linked her fingers with his. "I'm sorrier that I'm going to have to go up and work, at least for a few hours."

"Got a minute first?"

"Yeah, maybe. Just." And she let him pull her down into his lap. Let herself close her eyes and simply wallow there, in the scent and the feel of him. "Not exactly the kind of day you'd planned."

"That's what I get for marrying a cop." Ireland sang quietly in his voice, the lilt of a sexy poet. "For loving one," he added, and tipped her face up to kiss her.

"It's a pretty lousy deal right now."

"Not from where I'm sitting." He combed his fingers through her short brown hair. "You're what I want, Eve, the woman who leaves her home to stand over the dead. And the one who knew what a copy of Yeats would mean to me."

"I'm better with the dead than with buying presents. Otherwise I'd have come up with more than one."

She looked over at the small mountain of gifts under the tree—gifts it had taken her more than an hour to open. And her wince made him laugh.

"You know, one of the greatest rewards in giving you presents, Lieutenant, is the baffled embarrassment they cause you."

"I hope you got it out of your system for a while."

"Mmm," was his only response. She wasn't used to gifts, he thought, hadn't been given anything as a child but pain. "Have you decided what to do with the last one?"

The final box he'd given her had been empty, and he'd enjoyed seeing her frown in puzzlement. Just as he'd enjoyed seeing her grin at him when he told her it was a day. A day she could fill with whatever she liked. He would take her wherever she wanted to go, and they would do whatever she wanted to do. Off-planet or on. In reality or through the holo-room.

Any time, any place, any world was hers for the asking.

"No, I haven't had much time to think it through. It's a pretty great gift. I don't want to screw it up."

She let herself relax against him another moment with the fire crackling, the tree shimmering, then she pulled back. "I've got to get started. There's a lot of drone work on this one, and I don't want to tag Peabody today."

"Why don't I give you a hand?" He smiled again at the automatic refusal he read in her eyes. "Step into Peabody's sturdy shoes for the day."

"This one's not connected to you in any way. I want to keep it that way."

"All the better." He nudged her up, got to his feet. "I can help you do the runs or whatever, and that way you won't have to spend your entire Christmas chained to your desk.''

She started to refuse again, then reconsidered. Most of the data she wanted were public domain in any case. And what wasn't was nothing she wouldn't have shared with him if she'd been thinking it through aloud.

Besides, he was good.

''Okay, consider yourself a drone. But when Peabody's got her balance, you're out.''

''Darling.'' He took her hand, kissed it, watched her scowl. ''Since you ask so sweetly.''

''And no sloppy stuff,'' she put in. ''I'm on duty.''

TWO

The huge cat, Galahad, was draped over the back of Eve's sleep chair like a drunk over a bar at last call. Since he'd spent several hours the night before attacking boxes, fighting with ribbon, and murdering discarded wrapping paper, she left him where he was so he could sleep it off.

Eve set down her bag and went directly to the AutoChef for coffee. "The guy we're after is David Palmer."

"You've already identified the killer."

"Oh, yeah, I know who I'm after. Me and Dave, we're old pals."

Roarke took the mug she brought him, watched her through the steam. "The name's vaguely familiar to me."

"You'd have heard it. It was all over the media three, three and a half years ago. I need all my case files on that investigation, all data on the trial. You can start by—" She broke off when he laid a hand on her arm.

"David Palmer—serial killer. Torture murders." It was playing back for him, in bits and pieces. "Fairly young. What—mid-twenties?"

"Twenty-two at time of arrest. A real prodigy, our Dave.

9

He considers himself a scientist, a visionary. His mission is to explore and record the human mind's tolerance to extreme duress—pain, fear, starvation, dehydration, sensory deprivation. He could talk a good game, too." She sipped her coffee. "He'd sit there in interview, his pretty face all lit with enthusiasm, and explain that once we knew the mind's breaking point, we'd be able to enhance it, to strengthen it. He figured since I was a cop, I'd be particularly interested in his work. Cops are under a great deal of stress, often finding ourselves in life-and-death situations where the mind is easily distracted by fear or outside stimuli. The results of his work could be applied to members of the police and security forces, the military, even in business situations."

"I didn't realize he was yours."

"Yeah, he was mine." She shrugged her shoulders. "I was a little more low profile in those days."

He might have smiled at that, knowing it was partially her connection to him that had changed that status. But he remembered too much of the Palmer case to find the humor. "I was under the impression that he was safely locked away."

"Not safely enough. He slipped out. The victim this morning was dumped in a public area—another of Dave's trademarks. He likes us to know he's hard at work. The autopsy will have to verify, but the victim was tortured premortem. I'd guess Dave found himself a new hole to work in and had the judge there at least a day before killing him. Death by strangulation occurred on or around midnight. Merry Christmas, Judge Wainger," she murmured.

"And that would be the judge who tried his case."

"Yeah." Absently, she put her mug down, reached into her bag for a copy of the sealed note she'd already sent to the lab. "He left a calling card—another signature. All these names are connected to his case and his sentencing. Part of his work this time around would be, at my guess, letting his intended victims stew about what he has in store for them. They're being contacted and protected. He'll have a tough time getting to any of them."

"And you?" Roarke spoke with studied calm after a glance at the list, and his wife's name. "Where's your protection?"

"I'm a cop. I'm the one who does the protecting."

"He'll want you most, Eve."

She turned. However controlled his voice was, she heard the anger under it. "Maybe, but not as much as I want him."

"You stopped him," Roarke continued. "Whatever was done after—the tests, the trial, the sentence—was all a result of your work. You'll matter most."

"Let's leave those conclusions to the profiler." Though she agreed with them. "I'm going to contact Mira as soon as I look through the case files again. You can access those for me while I start my prelim report. I'll give you the codes for my office unit and the Palmer files."

Now he lifted a brow, smiled smugly. "Please. I can't work if you insult me."

"Sorry." She picked up her coffee again. "I don't know why I pretend you need codes to access any damn thing."

"Neither do I."

He sat down to retrieve the data she wanted, moving smoothly through the task. It was pitifully simple for him, and his mind was left free to consider. To decide.

She'd said he wasn't connected to this, and that she expected him to back away when Peabody was on duty again. But she was wrong. Her name on the list meant he was more involved than he'd ever been before. And no power on earth, not even that of the woman he loved, would cause him to back away.

Close by, Eve worked on the auxiliary unit, recording the stark facts into the report. She wanted the autopsy results, the crime scene team and sweeper data. But she had little hope that she would get anything from the spotty holiday staff before the end of the next day.

Struggling not to let her irritation with Christmas resurface, she answered her beeping 'link. "Dallas."

"Lieutenant, Officer Miller here."

"What is it, Miller?"

"Sir, my partner and I were assigned to contact and guard APA Ring. We arrived at her residence shortly after seven-thirty. There was no response to our knock."

"This is a priority situation, Miller. You're authorized to enter the premises."

"Yes, sir. Understood. We did so. The subject is not in residence. My partner questioned the across-the-hall neighbor. The subject left early yesterday morning to spend the holiday with her family in Philadelphia. Lieutenant, she never arrived. Her father reported her missing this morning."

Eve's stomach tightened. Too late, she thought. Already too late. "What was her method of transpo, Miller?"

"She had her own car. We're en route to the garage where she stored it."

"Keep me posted, Miller." Eve broke transmission, looked over, and met Roarke's eyes. "He's got her. I'd like to think she ran into some road hazard or hired a licensed companion for a quick holiday fling before heading on to her family, but he's got her. I need the 'link codes for the other names on the list."

"You'll have them. One minute."

She didn't need the code for one of the names. With her heart beating painfully, she put the call through to Mira's home. A small boy answered with a grin and a giggle. "Merry Christmas! This is Grandmom's house."

For a moment Eve just blinked, wondering how she'd gotten the wrong code. Then she heard the familiar soft voice in the background, saw Mira come on screen with a smile on her face and strain in her eyes.

"Eve. Good morning. Would you hold for a moment, please? I'd like to take this upstairs. No, sweetie," she said to the boy who tugged on her sleeve. "Run play with your new toys. I'll be back. Just a moment, Eve."

The screen went to a calm, cool blue, and Eve exhaled gratefully. Relief at finding Mira home, alive, well, safe— and the oddity of thinking of the composed psychiatrist as Grandmom played through her mind.

"I'm sorry." Mira came back on. "I didn't want to take this downstairs with my family."

"No problem. Are the uniforms there?"

"Yes." In a rare show of nerves, Mira pushed a hand through her sable-toned hair. "Miserable duty for them, sitting out in a car on Christmas. I haven't figured out how to have them inside and keep my family from knowing. My children are here, Eve, my grandchildren. I need to know if you believe there's any chance they're in danger."

"No." She said it quick and firm. "That's not his style. Dr. Mira, you're not to leave the house without your guards. You're to go nowhere, not the office, not the corner deli, without both of them. Tomorrow you'll be fitted for a tracer bracelet."

"I'll take all the precautions, Eve."

"Good, because one of those precautions is to cancel all patient appointments until Palmer is in custody."

"That's ridiculous."

"You're to be alone with no one, at any time. So unless your patients agree to let you walk around in their heads while a couple of cops are looking on, you're taking a vacation."

Mira eyed Eve steadily. "And are you about to take a vacation?"

"I'm about to do my job. Part of that job is you. Stephanie Ring is missing." She waited, one beat only, for the implication to register. "Do what you're told, Dr. Mira, or you'll be in protective custody within the hour. I'll need a consult tomorrow, nine o'clock. I'll come to you."

She broke transmission, turned to get the 'link codes from Roarke, and found him watching her steadily. "What?"

"She means a great deal to you. If she meant less, you'd have handled that with more finesse."

"I don't have much finesse at the best of times. Let's have the codes." When he hesitated, she sighed and replied, "Okay, okay, fine. She means a lot, and I'll be damned if he'll get within a mile of her. Now give me the goddamn codes."

"Already transferred to your unit, Lieutenant. Logged in, on memory. You've only to state the name of the party for transmission."

"Show-off." She muttered it, knowing it would make him grin, and turned back to contact the rest of the names on Palmer's list.

When she was satisfied that the other targets were where they were supposed to be, and under guard, Eve turned to the case files Roarke had accessed.

She spent an hour going over data and reports, another reviewing her interview discs with Palmer.

Okay, Dave, tell me about Michelle Hammel. What made her special?

David Palmer, a well-built man of twenty-two with the golden good looks of the wealthy New England family he'd sprung from, smiled and leaned forward earnestly. His clear blue eyes were bright with enthusiasm. His caramel-cream complexion glowed with health and vitality.

Somebody's finally listening, Eve remembered thinking as she saw herself as she'd been three years before. *He's finally got the chance to share his genius.*

Her hair was badly cut—she'd still been hacking at it herself in those days. The boots crossed at her ankles had been new then and almost unscarred. There was no wedding ring on her finger.

Otherwise, she thought, she was the same.

She was young, fit. An athlete, Palmer told her. *Very disciplined, mind and body. A long-distance runner—Olympic hopeful. She knew how to block pain, how to focus on a goal. She'd be at the top end of the scale, you see. Just as Leroy Greene was at the bottom. He'd fogged his mind with illegals for years. No tolerance for disruptive stimuli. He lost all control even before the application of pain. His mind broke as soon as he regained consciousness and found himself strapped to the table. But Michelle . . .*

She fought? She held out?

Palmer nodded cheerfully. *She was magnificent, really. She struggled against the restraints, then stopped when she understood that she wouldn't be able to free herself. There was fear. The monitors registered her rise in pulse rate, blood pressure, all vital physical and emotional signs. I have excellent equipment.*

Yeah, I've seen it. Top of the line.

It's vital work. His eyes had clouded then, unfocused as they did when he spoke of the import of his experiments. *You'll see if you review the data on Michelle that she centered her fear, used it to keep herself alive. She controlled it, initially, tried to reason with me. She made promises, she pretended to understand my research, even to help me. She was clever. When she understood that wouldn't help her, she cursed me, pumping up her adrenaline as I introduced new pain stimuli.*

"He broke her feet," Eve said, knowing Roarke was watching behind her. "Then her arms. He was right about his equipment back then. He had electrodes that when attached to different parts of the body, or placed in various orifices, administered graduating levels of electric shock. He kept Michelle alive for three days until the torture broke her. She was begging for him to kill her toward the end. He used a rope and pulley system to hang her—gradual strangulation. She was nineteen."

Roarke laid his hands on her shoulders. "You stopped him once, Eve, you'll stop him again."

"Damn right I will."

She looked up when she heard someone coming quickly down the corridor. "Save data, and file," she ordered just as Nadine Furst came into the room. Perfect, she thought, a visit from one of Channel 75's top on-air reporters. The fact that they were friends didn't make Eve any less wary.

"Out paying Christmas calls, Nadine?"

"I got a present this morning." Nadine tossed a disc on the desk.

Eve looked at it, then back up at Nadine's face. It was pale, the sharp features drawn. For once, Nadine wasn't perfectly groomed with lip dye, enhancers, and every hair in place. She looked more than frazzled, Eve realized. She looked afraid.

"What's the problem?"

"David Palmer."

Slowly Eve got to her feet. "What about him?"

"Apparently he knows what I do for a living, and that we're friendly. He sent me that." She glanced back down at the disc, struggled to suppress a shudder. "Hoping I'd do a feature story on him—and his work—and share the contents of his disc with you. Can I have a drink? Something strong."

Roarke came around the desk and eased her into a chair. "Sit down. You're cold," he murmured when he took her hands.

"Yeah, I am. I've been cold ever since I ran that disc."

"I'll get you a brandy."

Nadine nodded in agreement, then fisted her hands in her lap and looked at Eve. "There are two other people on the recording. One of them is Judge Wainger. What's left of Judge Wainger. And there's a woman, but I can't recognize her. She's—he's already started on her."

"Here." Roarke brought the snifter, gently wrapped Nadine's hands around the bowl. "Drink this."

"Okay." She lifted the glass, took one long sip, and felt the blast of heat explode in her gut. "Dallas, I've seen a lot of bad things. I've reported them, I've studied them. But I've never seen anything like this. I don't know how you deal with it, day after day."

"One day at a time." Eve picked up the disc. "You don't have to watch this again."

"Yes." Nadine drank again, let out a long breath. "I do."

Eve turned the disc over in her hand. It was a standard-use model. They'd never trace it. She slid it into her unit. "Copy disc and run, display on screen."

David Palmer's youthful and handsome face swam onto the wall screen.

"Ms. Furst, or may I call you Nadine? So much more personal that way, and my work is very personal to me. I've admired your work, by the way. It's one of the reasons I'm trusting you to get my story on air. You believe in what you do, don't you, Nadine?"

His eyes were serious now, professional to professional, his face holding all the youth and innocence of a novitiate at the altar. "Those of us who reach for perfection believe in what we do," he continued. "I'm aware that you have a friendly relationship with Lieutenant Dallas. The lieutenant and I also have a relationship, perhaps not so friendly, but we do connect, and I do admire her stamina. I hope you'll share the contents of this disc with her as soon as possible. By this time she should already be heading the investigation into the death of Judge Wainger."

His smile went bright now, and just a little mad at the edges. "Hello, Lieutenant. You'll excuse me if I just conclude my business with Nadine. I want Dallas to be closely involved. It's important to me. You will tell my story, won't you, Nadine? Let the public themselves judge, not some narrow-minded fool in a black robe."

The next scene slipped seamlessly into place, the audio high so that the woman's screams seemed to rip the air in the room where Eve sat, watching.

Judge Wainger's body was bound hand and foot and suspended several inches from a plain concrete floor. A basic pulley system this time, Eve mused. He'd taken time to set up some of the niceties, but it wasn't yet the complex, and yes, ingenious, system of torture that he'd created before.

Still, he worked very well.

Wainger's face was livid with agony, the muscles twitching as Palmer burned letters in his chest with a hand laser. He only moaned, his head lolling. Nearby, a system of monitors beeped and buzzed.

"He's failing, you see," Palmer said briskly in a voice-over. "His mind is moving beyond the pain, as it can no longer endure it. His system will attempt to shut down into unconsciousness. That can be reversed, as you'll see here." On screen, he flipped a switch. There was a high whine, then Wainger's body jerked. This time he screamed.

Across the room a woman shrieked and sobbed. The cage she was in swung wildly on its cable and was only big enough to allow her to crouch on hands and knees. A dark fall of hair covered most of her face, but Eve knew her.

Stephanie Ring was Palmer's.

When he turned, engaged another control, the cage sparked and shook. The woman let out a piercing wail, shuddered convulsively, then collapsed.

Palmer turned to the camera, smiled. "She's distracting, but I have only so much time. It's necessary to begin one subject before completing work on another. But her turn will come shortly. Subject Wainger's heart is failing. The data on him are nearly complete."

Using the ropes, he manually lowered Wainger to the floor. Eve noted the flex and bunch of muscles in Palmer's arms. "Dave's been pumping," she murmured. "Getting in shape. He knew he'd have to work harder this round. He likes to prepare."

Palmer slipped a perfectly knotted noose around Wainger's neck and meticulously slid the trailing end through a metal ring in the ceiling. Leading it down, he threaded it through another ring in the floor, then pulled out the slack until Wainger rose to his knees, then his feet, and began gasping for air.

"Stop it, will you?" Nadine leapt to her feet. "I can't watch this again. I thought I could. I can't."

"Stop disc." Eve waited until the screen went blank, then went over to crouch in front of Nadine. "I'm sorry."

"No. I'm sorry. I thought I was tough."

"You are. Nobody's this tough."

Nadine shook her head and, finishing her brandy with one deep gulp, set the snifter aside. "You are. You don't let it get to you."

"It gets to me. But this is for me. I'm going to have a couple of uniforms come and take you home. They're going to hang with you everywhere until Palmer's down."

"You think he'll come after me?"

"No, but why take chances? Go home, Nadine. Put it away."

But after she'd asked Roarke to take Nadine downstairs to wait for the escort, Eve finished watching the disc. And at the end her eyes met Palmer's as he moved toward the camera.

"Subject Wainger died at midnight, December twenty-fourth. You'll last longer, Dallas. We both know that. You'll be my most fascinating subject. I have such wonders planned for you. You'll find me. I know you will. I'm counting on it. Happy holidays."

THREE

Stephanie Ring's car was still in its permit slot in the garage. Her luggage was neatly stowed in the trunk. Eve circled the vehicle, searching for any sign of struggle, any evidence that might have been dropped and gone unnoticed during the snatch.

"He's got two basic MOs," she said, as much to herself as to the uniforms waiting nearby. "One is to gain entrance into the victims' homes by a ruse—delivery, repair, or service con; the other is to come on them in an unpopulated area. He spends time getting to know their routines and habits, the usual routes and schedules. He keeps all that in a log—very organized, scientific, along with bio data on each of them."

They weren't lab rats to him, she mused. It was personal, individualized. That was what excited him.

"In either case," she went on, "he uses a stunner, takes them down quickly, then transports them in his own vehicle. Security cameras operational in here?"

"Yes, sir." One of the uniforms passed her a sealed package of discs. "We confiscated them for the last three days, assuming that the subject may have stalked the victim previous to her abduction.''

Eve lifted a brow. ''Miller, right?''

''Sir.''

''Good thinking. There's nothing more you can do here. Go home and eat some goose.''

They didn't exactly race away, but neither did they linger. Eve put the package in her bag and turned to Roarke. ''Why don't you do the same, pal? I'll only be a couple of hours.''

''We'll only be a couple of hours.''

''I don't need an aide to do a pass through Ring's apartment.''

Roarke simply took her arm and led her back to the car. ''You let the two uniforms go,'' he began as he started the engine. ''Everyone else on Palmer's list is under guard. Why aren't you?''

''We covered that already.''

''Partially.'' He reversed and headed out of the garage. ''But I know you, Lieutenant. You're hoping he'll shuffle the order and come after you next. And you don't want some big-shouldered uniforms scaring him off.''

For a moment she just drummed her fingers on her knee. In less than a year, the man had learned her inside and out. She wasn't entirely comfortable with that. ''And your point would be?''

He nearly smiled at the annoyance in her voice. ''I admire my wife's courage, her dedication to duty.''

''You tossed in 'my wife' to irritate me, didn't you?''

''Of course.'' Satisfied, he picked up her hand, kissed the knuckles. ''I'm sticking, Eve. Deal with it.''

The pass through Stephanie Ring's apartment was no more than routine, and it turned up nothing but the tidy life of a single career woman who enjoyed surrounding herself with attractive things, spending her city salary on a stylish wardrobe.

Eve thought of the naked woman crouched like an animal in a cage, screaming in terror.

He's killing her now. Eve knew it. And she had no power to stop him.

When she was back in her home office, she reviewed the disc Palmer had sent Nadine. This time she willed herself to ignore what was happening and focus only on the surroundings.

"No windows," she commented. "The floor and walls look like concrete and old brick. The whole area can't be over thirty feet by twenty. It's probably a basement. Computer, pause. Enhance sector eight through fifteen. Magnify."

She paced as the computer went to work, then moved closer to the screen. "There, that's a stair tread. Steps, part of a railing. Behind it is some sort of—what is it—old furnace unit or water tank. He's found himself a hole. It has to be private," she continued, studying the view. "He can't do his work in a building where people might hear. Even if it's soundproofed, he'd risk someone poking around. Maintenance crew, repair team. Anything like that."

"Not an apartment or office building," Roarke agreed. "And with the steps it's not likely a storage facility. From the look of the furnace, it's a good-sized building, but far from new. Nothing built in the last fifteen or twenty years would have had a tank furnace installed. He'd want something in the city, wouldn't he?"

"Yeah, he'd want to be close to all of his marks. He wouldn't go for the 'burbs and even the boroughs aren't likely. Dave's a true urbanite and New York's his turf. Private home. Has to be. But how did he get his hands on a private residence?"

"Friends?" Roarke suggested. "Family?"

"Palmer didn't have a tight circle of friends. He's a loner. He has parents. They relocated after the trial. Went under the Victim and Survivor's Protection Act."

"Sealed files."

She heard the faintest trace of humor in his voice, turned to scowl at him. For a moment she wrestled with procedure. She could get clearance to access the Palmers' location.

And it would take at least two days to hack through the red tape for authorization. Or she could hand the problem to Roarke and have what she needed in minutes.

She could hear Stephanie Ring's screams echoing in her head.

"You'll have to use the unregistered equipment. Compuguard will have an automatic block on their file."

"It won't take long."

"I'm going to keep working on this." She gestured toward the screen. "He might have slipped up just enough to have let something identifiable come through."

"All right." But he crossed to her, framed her face in his hands. Lowering his head, he kissed her, long and slow and deep. And felt, as he did, some of the rigid tension in her body ease.

"I can handle this, Roarke."

"Whether you can or not, you will. Would it hurt to hold on to me, just for a minute?"

"Guess not." She slipped her arms around him, felt the familiar lines, the familiar warmth. Her grip tightened. "Why wasn't it enough to stop him once? Why wasn't it enough to put him away? What good is it if you do your job and it comes back this way?"

He held her and said nothing.

"He wants to show me he can do it all again. He wants to take me through all the steps and stages, the way he did before. Only this time as they're happening. 'Look how clever I am, Dallas.' "

"Knowing that, understanding that, will help you stop him a second time."

"Yeah." She eased back. "Get me the data so I can hammer at his parents."

Roarke skimmed a finger over the dent in her chin. "You'll let me watch, won't you. It's so stimulating to see you browbeat witnesses."

When she laughed, as he'd hoped she would, he went to his private room to circumvent Compuguard and officially sealed files.

She'd barely had time to review another section of the recording before he came back.

"It couldn't have been that easy."

"Yes." He smiled and passed her a new data disc. "It could. Thomas and Helen Palmer, now known as Thomas and Helen Smith—which shows just how imaginative bureaucrats can be, currently reside in a small town called Leesboro in rural Pennsylvania."

"Pennsylvania." Eve glanced toward her 'link, considered, then looked back at Roarke. "It wouldn't take long to get there if you had access to some slick transpo."

Roarke looked amused. "Which slick transpo would you prefer, Lieutenant?"

"That mini-jet of yours would get us there in under an hour."

"Then why don't we get started?"

If Eve had been more fond of heights, she might have enjoyed the fast, smooth flight south. As it was, she sat, jiggling a foot to relieve a case of nerves while Roarke piloted them over what she imagined some would consider a picturesque range of mountains.

To her they were just rocks, and the fields between them just dirt.

"I'm only going to say this once," she began. "And only because it's Christmas."

"Banking for landing," he warned her as he approached the private airstrip. "What are you only going to say once?"

"That maybe all these toys of yours aren't a complete waste of time. Overindulgent, maybe, but not a complete waste of time."

"Darling, I'm touched."

Once they were on the ground, they transferred from the snazzy little two-person jet to the car that Roarke had waiting. Of course, it couldn't be a normal vehicle, Eve mused as she studied it. It was a sleek black bullet of a car, built for style and speed.

"I'll drive." She held out a hand for the keycode the attendant had given him. "You navigate."

Roarke considered her as he tossed the code in his hand. "Why?"

"Because I'm the one with the badge." She snatched the code on its upward arc and smirked at him.

"I'm a better driver."

She snorted as they climbed in. "You like to hotdog. That doesn't make you better. Strap in, ace. I'm in a hurry."

She punched it and sent them flying away from the terminal and onto a winding rural road that was lined with snow-laced trees and sheer rock.

Roarke programmed their destination and studied the route offered by the onboard computer. "Follow this road for two miles, turn left for another ten point three, then next left for five point eight."

By the time he'd finished, she was already making the first left. She spotted a narrow creek, water fighting its way through ice, over rock. A scatter of houses, trees climbing steeply up hills, a few children playing with new airskates or boards in snow-covered yards.

"Why do people live in places like this? There's nothing here. You see all that sky?" she asked Roarke. "You shouldn't be able to see that much sky from down here. It can't be good for you. And where do they eat? We haven't passed a single restaurant, glide cart, deli, nothing."

"Cozily?" Roarke suggested. "Around the kitchen table."

"All the time? Jesus." She shuddered.

He laughed, smoothed a finger over her hair. "Eve, I adore you."

"Right." She tapped the brakes to make the next turn. "What am I looking for?"

"Third house on the right. There, that two-story prefab, mini-truck in the drive."

She slowed, scanning the house as she turned in behind the truck. There were Christmas lights along the eaves, a wreath on the door, and the outline of a decorated tree behind the front window.

"No point in asking you to wait in the car, I guess."

"None," he agreed and got out.

"They're not going to be happy to see me," Eve warned him as they crossed the shoveled walk to the front door. "If they refuse to talk to me, I'm going to give them some hard shoves. If it comes down to it, you just follow the lead."

She pressed the buzzer, shivered.

"You should have worn the coat I gave you. Cashmere's warm."

"I'm not wearing that on duty." It was gorgeous, she thought. And made her feel soft. It wasn't the sort of thing that worked for a cop.

And when the door opened, Eve was all cop.

Helen Palmer had changed her hair and her eyes. Subtle differences in shades and shapes, but enough to alter her looks. It was still a pretty face, very like her son's. Her automatic smile of greeting faded as she recognized Eve.

"You remember me, Mrs. Palmer?"

"What are you doing here?" Helen put a hand high on the doorjamb as if to block it. "How did you find us? We're under protection."

"I don't intend to violate that. I have a crisis situation. You'd have been informed that your son has escaped from prison."

Helen pressed her lips together, hunched her shoulders as a defense against the cold that whipped through the open door. "They said they were looking for him, assured us that they'd have him back in custody, back in treatment very soon. He isn't here. He doesn't know where we are."

"Can I come in, Mrs. Palmer?"

"Why do you have to rake this all up again?" Tears swam into her eyes, seeming as much from frustration as grief. "My husband and I are just getting our lives back. We've had no contact with David in nearly three years."

"Honey? Who's at the door? You're letting the cold in." A tall man with a dark sweep of hair came smiling to the door. He wore an old cardigan sweater and ancient jeans with a pair of obviously new slippers. He blinked once,

twice, then laid his hand on his wife's shoulder. "Lieutenant. Lieutenant Dallas, isn't it?"

"Yes, Mr. Palmer. I'm sorry to disturb you."

"Let them in, Helen."

"Oh, God, Tom."

"Let them in." His fingers rubbed over her shoulder before he drew her back. "You must be Roarke." Tom
worked up what nearly passed·for a smile as he offered
Roarke his hand. "I recognize you. Please come in and sit
down."

"Tom, please—"

"Why don't you make some coffee?" He turned and
pressed his lips to his wife's brow. He murmured something
to her, and she let out a shuddering breath and nodded.

"I'll make this as quick as I can, Mr. Palmer," Eve told
him, as Helen walked quickly down a central hallway.

"You dealt very fairly with us during an unbearable
time, Lieutenant." He showed them into a small living area.
"I haven't forgotten that. Helen—my wife's been on edge
all day. For several days," he corrected himself. "Since we
were informed that David escaped. We've worked very
hard to keep that out of the center, but . . ."

He gestured helplessly and sat down.

Eve remembered these decent people very well, their
shock and grief over what their son was. They had raised
him with love, with discipline, with care, and still they had
been faced with a monster.

There had been no abuse, no cruelty, no underlying gruel
for that monster to feed on. Mira's testing and analysis had
corroborated Eve's impression of a normal couple who'd
given their only child their affection and the monetary and
social advantages that had been at their disposal.

"I don't have good news for you, Mr. Palmer. I don't
have easy·news."

He folded his hands in his lap. "He's dead."

"No."

Tom closed his eyes. "God help me. I'd hoped—I'd actually hoped he was." He got up quickly when he heard
his wife coming back. "Here, I'll take that." He bent to

take the tray she carried. "We'll get through this, Helen."

"I know. I know we will." She came in, sat, busied herself pouring the coffee she'd made. "Lieutenant, do you think David's come back to New York?"

"We know he has." She hesitated, then decided they would hear the news soon enough through the media. "Early this morning the body of Judge Wainger was found in Rockefeller Plaza. It's David's work," she continued as Helen moaned. "He's contacted me, with proof. There's no doubt of it."

"He was supposed to be given treatment. Kept away from people so he couldn't hurt them, hurt himself."

"Sometimes the system fails, Mrs. Palmer. Sometimes you can do everything right, and it just fails."

Helen rose, walked to the window, and stood looking out. "You said something like that to me before. To us. That we'd done everything right, everything we could. That it was something in David that had failed. That was kind of you, Lieutenant, but you can't know what it's like, you can't know how it feels to know that a monster has come from you."

No, Eve thought, but she knew what it was to come from a monster, to have been raised by one for the first eight years of her life. And she lived with it.

"I need your help," she said instead. "I need you to tell me if you have any idea where he might go, who he might go to. He has a place," she continued. "A private place where he can work. A house, a small building somewhere in New York. In the city or very close by."

"He has nowhere." Tom lifted his hands. "We sold everything when we relocated. Our home, my business, Helen's. Even our holiday place in the Hamptons. We cut all ties. The house where David—where he lived that last year—was sold as well. We live quietly here, simply. The money we'd accumulated, the money from the sales is sitting in an account. We haven't had the heart to . . . we don't need it."

"He had money of his own," Eve prompted.

"Yes, inheritance, a trust fund. It was how he financed

what he was doing." Tom reached out a hand for his wife's and clasped her fingers tightly. "We donated that money to charity. Lieutenant, all the places where he might have gone are in the hands of others now."

"All right. You may think of something later. However far-fetched, please contact me." She rose. "When David's in custody again, I'll let you know. After that, I'll forget where you are."

Eve said nothing more until she and Roarke were in the car and headed back. "They still love him. After all he did, after what he is, there's a part of them that loves him."

"Yes, and enough, I think, to help you stop him, if they knew how."

"No one ever cared for us that way." She took her eyes off the road briefly, met his. "No one ever felt that bond."

"No." He brushed the hair from her cheek. "Not until we found each other. Don't grieve, Eve."

"He has his mother's eyes," she murmured. "Soft and blue and clear. She's the one who had to change them, I imagine, because she couldn't look in the mirror and face them every morning."

She sighed, shook it off.

"But he can," she said quietly.

FOUR

There was nothing else to do, no other data to examine or analyze, no other route to check. Tomorrow, she knew, there would be. Now she could only wait.

Eve walked into the bedroom with some idea of taking a catnap. They needed to salvage some of the day, she thought. To have their Christmas dinner together, to squeeze in some sense of normalcy.

The strong, dreamy scent of pine made her shake her head. The man had gone wild for tradition on this, their first Christmas together. Christ knew what he had paid for the live trees he'd placed throughout the house. And this one, the one that stood by the window in their bedroom, he'd insisted they decorate together.

It mattered to him. And with some surprise she realized it had come to matter to her.

"Tree lights on," she ordered, and smiled a little as she watched them blink and flash.

She stepped toward the seating area, released her weapon harness, and shrugged it off. She was sitting on the arm of the sofa taking off her boots when Roarke came in.

"Good. I was hoping you'd take a break. I've got some calls to make. Why don't you let me know when you're ready for a meal?"

She angled her head and studied him as he stood just inside the doorway. She let her second boot drop and stood up slowly. "Come here."

Recognizing the glint in her eyes, he felt the light tingle of lust begin to move through his blood. "There?"

"You heard me, slick."

Keeping his eyes on hers he walked across the room. "What can I do for you, Lieutenant?"

Traditions, Eve thought, had to start somewhere. She fisted a hand in the front of his shirt, straining the silk as she pulled him a step closer. "I want you naked, and quick. So unless you want me to get rough, strip."

His smile was as cocky as hers and made her want to sink in with her teeth. "Maybe I like it rough."

"Yeah?" She began to back him up toward the bed. "Well then, you're going to love this."

She moved fast, the only signal was the quick flash of her eyes before she ripped his shirt open and sent buttons flying. He gripped her hips, squeezing hard as she fixed her teeth on his shoulder and bit.

"Christ. Christ! I love your body. Give it to me."

"You want it?" He jerked her up to her toes. "You'll have to take it."

When his mouth would have closed hotly over hers, she pivoted. He countered. She came in low and might have flipped him if he hadn't anticipated her move. They'd gone hand to hand before, with very satisfying results.

They ended face-to-face again, breath quickening. "I'm taking you down," she warned him.

"Try it."

They grappled, both refusing to give way. The momentum took them up the stairs of the platform to the bed. She slipped a hand between his legs, gently squeezed. It was a move she'd used before. Even as the heat shot straight down the center of his body to her palm, he shifted, slid under her guard, and flipped her onto the bed.

She rolled, came up in a crouch. "Come on, tough guy."

She was grinning now, her face flushed with battle, desire going gold in her eyes and the lights of the tree sparkling behind her.

"You look beautiful, Eve."

That had her blinking, straightening from the fighting stance and gaping at him. Even the man who loved her had never accused her of beauty. "Huh?"

It was all she managed before he leapt at her and took her out with a mid-body tackle.

"Bastard." She nearly giggled it even as she scissored up and managed to roll on top of him. But he used the impetus to keep going until he had her pinned again. "Beautiful, my ass."

"Your ass is beautiful." The elbow to his gut knocked some of the breath out of him, but he sucked more in. "And so's the rest of you. I'm going to have your beautiful ass, and the rest of you."

She bucked, twisted, nearly managed to slip out from under him. Then his mouth closed over her breast, sucking, nipping through her shirt. She moaned, arched up against him, and the fist she'd clenched in his hair dragged him closer rather than yanking him away.

When he tore at her shirt, she reared up, hooking strong, long legs around his waist, finding his mouth with hers again as he pushed back to kneel in the center of the bed.

They went over in a tangle of limbs, hands rough and groping. And flesh began to slide damply over flesh.

He took her up and over the first time, hard and fast, those clever fingers knowing her weaknesses, her strengths, her needs. Quivering, crying out, she let herself fly on the edgy power of the climax.

Then they were rolling again, gasps and moans and murmurs. Heat coming in tidal waves, nerves raw and needy. Her mouth was a fever on his as she straddled him.

"Let me, let me, let me." She chanted it against his mouth as she rose up. Her hands linked tight to his as she took him inside her. He filled her, body, mind, heart.

Fast and full of fury, she drove them both as she'd needed to from the moment he'd come into the room. It flooded into her, swelled inside her, that unspeakable pleasure, the pressure, the frantic war to end, to prolong.

She threw her head back, clung to it, that razor's edge.
"Go over." She panted it out, fighting to clear her vision,
to focus on that glorious face. "Go over first, and take me
with you."

She watched his eyes, that staggering blue go dark as
midnight, felt him leap over with one last, hard thrust. With
her hands still locked in his, she threw herself over with
him.

And when the energy slid away from her like wax from
a melting candle, she slipped down, quivering even as she
pressed her face into his neck.

"I won," she managed.

"Okay."

Her lips twitched at the smug, and exhausted, satisfaction
in his voice. "I did. I got just what I wanted from you,
pal."

"Thank Christ." He shifted until he could cradle her
against him. "Take a nap, Eve."

"Just an hour." Knowing he would never sleep longer
than that himself, she wrapped around him to keep him
close.

When she woke at two A.M., Eve decided the brief predinner nap had thrown her system off. Now she was fully
awake, her mind engaged and starting to click through the
information and evidence she had so far.

David Palmer was here, in New York. Somewhere out
in the city, happily going about his work. And her gut told
her Stephanie Ring was already dead.

He wouldn't have such an easy time getting to the others
on his list, she thought as she turned in bed. Ego would
push him to try, and he'd make a mistake. In all likelihood
he'd already made one. She just hadn't picked up on it yet.

Closing her eyes, she tried to slip into Palmer's mind, as
she had years before when she'd been hunting him.

He loved his work, had loved it even when he'd been a
boy and doing his experiments on animals. He'd managed

to hide those little deaths, to put on a bright, innocent face. Everyone who'd known him—parents, teachers, neighbors—had spoken of a cheerful, helpful boy, a bright one who studied hard and caused no trouble.

Yet some of the classic elements had been there, even in childhood. He'd been a loner, obsessively neat, compulsively organized. He'd never had a healthy sexual relationship and had been socially awkward with women. They'd found hundreds of journal discs, going back to his tenth year, carefully relating his theories, his goals, and his accomplishments.

And with time, with practice, with study, he'd gotten very, very good at his work.

Where would you set up, Dave? It would have to be somewhere comfortable. You like your creature comforts. You must have hated the lack of them in prison. Pissed you off, didn't it? So now you're coming after the ones who put you there.

That's a mistake, letting us know the marks in advance. But it's ego, too. It's really you against me.

That's another mistake, because no one knows you better.

A house, she thought. But not just any house. It would have to be in a good neighborhood, close to good restaurants. Those years of prison food must have offended your palate. You'd need furniture, comfortable stuff, with some style. Linens, good ones. And an entertainment complex—got to watch the screen or you won't know what people are saying about you.

And all that takes money.

When she sat up in bed, Roarke stirred beside her. "Figure it out?"

"He's got a credit line somewhere. I always wondered if he had money stashed, but it didn't seem to matter since he was never getting out to use it. I was wrong. Money's power, and he found a way to use it from prison."

She tossed back the duvet, started to leap out of bed when the 'link beeped. She stared at it a moment, and knew.

FIVE

Two teenagers looking for a little adventure snuck out of their homes, met at a prearranged spot, and took their new scoot-bikes for a spin in Central Park.

They'd thought at first that Stephanie Ring was a vagrant, maybe a licensed beggar or a chemi-head sleeping it off, and they started to give her a wide berth.

But vagrants didn't make a habit of stretching out naked on the carousel in Central Park.

Eve had both of them stashed in a black-and-white. One had been violently ill, and the brittle air still carried the smear of vomit. She'd ordered the uniforms to set up a stand of lights so the area was under the glare of a false day.

Stephanie hadn't been beaten, nor had her hair been cut. Palmer believed in variety. There were dozens of long, thin slices over her arms and legs, the flesh around the wounds shriveled and discolored. Something toxic, Eve imagined, something that when placed on a relatively minor open wound would cause agony. The blood had been allowed to drip and dry. Her feet speared out at sharp angles, in a parody of a ballet stance. Dislocated.

Carved into her midriff were the signature block letters.

LET'S KILL ALL THE LAWYERS

He had finally killed this one, Eve thought, with the slow, torturous strangulation he was most fond of. Eve examined the noose, found the rope identical to that used on Judge Wainger.

Another mistake, Dave. Lots of little oversights this time around.

She reached for her field kit and began the routine that followed murder.

She went home to write her report, wanting the quiet she'd find there as opposed to the postholiday confusion at Central. She shot a copy to her commander, then sent messages to both Peabody and Feeney. Once her aide and the top man in the Electronics Detective Division woke and checked their 'links, she was pulling them in.

She fueled on coffee, then set about the tedious task of peeling the layers from Palmer's financial records.

It was barely dawn when the door between her office and Roarke's opened. He came in, fully dressed, and she could hear the hum of equipment already at work in the room behind him.

"You working at home today?" she said it casually, sipping coffee as she studied him.

"Yes." He glanced down at her monitor. "Following the money, Lieutenant?"

"At the moment. You're not my bodyguard, Roarke."

He merely smiled. "And who, I wonder, could be more interested in your body?"

"I'm a cop. I don't need a sitter."

He reached down, cupped her chin. "What nearly happened to Peabody two nights ago?"

"It didn't happen. And I'm not having you hovering around when you should be off doing stuff."

"I can do stuff from here just as easily and efficiently as I can from midtown. You're wasting time arguing. And I doubt you'll find your money trail through Palmer's official records."

"I know it." The admission covered both statements, and frustrated her equally. "I have to start somewhere. Go away and let me work."

"Done with me, are you?" He lowered his head and brushed his lips over hers.

The sound of a throat being loudly and deliberately cleared came from the doorway. "Sorry." Peabody managed most of a smile. She was pale, and more than a little heavy-eyed, but her uniform was stiff and polished, as always.

"You're early." Eve rose, then slid her hands awkwardly into her pockets.

"The message said to report as soon as possible."

"I'll leave you two to work." Alone, Roarke thought, the two of them would slip past the discomfort faster. "It's good to see you, Peabody. Lieutenant," he added before he closed the door between the rooms, "you might want to check the names of deceased relatives. The transfer and disbursement of funds involving accounts with the same last name and blood ties are rarely noticed."

"Yeah, right. Thanks." Eve shifted her feet. The last time she'd seen her aide, Peabody had been wrapped in a blanket, her face blotchy from tears. "You okay?"

"Yeah, mostly."

Mostly, my ass, Eve thought. "Look, I shouldn't have called you in on this. Take a couple of more days to level off."

"Sir. I'd do better if I got back to work, into routine. Sitting home watching videos and eating soy chips isn't the way I want to spend another day. Work clears it out quicker."

Because she believed that herself, Eve moved her shoulders. "Then get some coffee, Peabody, I've got plenty of work here."

"Yes, sir." She stepped forward, pulling a small

wrapped box from her pocket, setting it on the desk as she went to the AutoChef. "Your Christmas present. I didn't get a chance to give it to you before."

"I guess we were a little busy." Eve toyed with the ribbon. Gifts always made her feel odd, but she could sense Peabody's eyes on her. She ripped off the red foil, opened the lid. It was a silver star, a little dented, a bit discolored.

"It's an old sheriff's badge," Peabody told her. "I don't guess it's like Wyatt Earp's or anything, but it's official. I thought you'd get a kick out of it. You know, the long tradition of law and order."

Absurdly touched, Eve grinned. "Yeah. It's great." For the fun of it, she took it out and pinned it to her shirt. "Does this make you the deputy?"

"It suits you, Dallas. You'd've stood up wherever, whenever."

Looking up, Eve met her eyes. "You stand, Peabody. I wouldn't have called you in today if I thought different."

"I guess I needed to hear that. Thanks. Well . . ." She hesitated, then lifted her brows in question.

"Problem?"

"No, I just . . ." She pouted, giving her square, sober face a painfully young look. "Hmmm."

"You didn't like your present?" Eve said lightly. "You'll have to take that up with Leonardo."

"What present? What's he got to do with it?"

"He made that wardrobe for your undercover work. If you don't like it . . ."

"The clothes." Like magic, Peabody's face cleared. "I get to keep all those mag clothes? All of them?"

"What the hell am I supposed to do with them? Now are you going to stand around grinning like an idiot or can I get on with things here?"

"I can grin and work at the same time, sir."

"Settle down. Start a run and trace on this rope." She pushed a hard-copy description across the desk. "I want any sales within the last week, bulk sales. He uses a lot of it."

"Who?"

"We'll get to that. Run the rope, then get me a list of private residences—upscale—sold or rented in the metro area within the last week. Also private luxury vehicles—pickup or delivery on those within the last week. He needs transpo and he'd go classy. The cage," she muttered as she began to pace. "Where the hell did he get the cage? Wildlife facility, domestic animal detention? We'll track it. Start the runs, Peabody, I'll brief you when Feeney gets here."

She'd called in Feeney, Peabody thought as she sat down at a computer. It was big. Just what she needed.

"You'll both want to review the investigation discs, profiles, transcripts from the Palmer case of three years ago. Feeney," Eve added, "you'll remember most of it. You tracked and identified the electronic equipment he used in those murders."

"Yeah, I remember the little bastard." Feeney sat, scowling into his coffee. His habitually weary face was topped by wiry red hair that never seemed to decide which direction it wanted to take.

He was wearing a blue shirt, so painfully pressed and bright that Eve imagined it had come out of its gift box only that morning. And would be comfortably rumpled by afternoon.

"Because we know him, his pattern, his motives, and in this case his victims or intended victims, he's given us an edge. He knows that, enjoys that because he's sure he'll be smarter."

"He hates you, Dallas." Feeney's droopy eyes lifted, met hers. "He hated your ever-fucking guts all along. You stopped him, then you played him until he spilled everything. He'll come hard for you."

"I hope you're right, because I want the pleasure of taking him out again. He got the first two on his list because he had a lead on us," she continued. "The others have been notified, warned, and are under guard. He may or may not make an attempt to continue in order. But once he runs into a snag, he'll skip down."

"And come for you," Peabody put in.

"Everything the others did happened because I busted him. Under the whack is a very logical mind. Everything he does has a reason. It's his reason, so it's bent—but it's there."

She glanced at her wrist unit. "I've got a meeting with Mira at her residence in twenty minutes. I'm going to leave it to Feeney to fill you in on any holes in this briefing, Peabody. Once you have the lists from the runs I ordered, do a probability scan. See if we can narrow the field a bit. Feeney, when you review the disc he sent through Nadine, you might be able to tag some of the equipment. You get a line on it, we can trace the source. We do it in steps, but we do it fast. If he misses on the list, he might settle for someone else, anyone else. He's been out a week and already killed twice."

She broke off as her communicator signaled. She walked to retrieve her jacket as she answered. Two minutes later she jammed it back in her pocket. And her eyes were flat and cold.

"Make that three times. He got to Carl Neissan."

Eve was still steaming when she rang the bell of Mira's dignified brownstone. The fact that the guard on door duty demanded that she show her ID and had it verified before entry mollified her slightly. If the man posted at Neissan's had done the same, Palmer wouldn't have gotten inside.

Mira came down the hall toward her. She was dressed casually in slacks and sweater, with soft matching shoes. But there was nothing casual about her eyes. Before Eve could speak, she lifted a hand.

"I appreciate your coming here. We can talk upstairs in my office." She glanced to the right as a child's laughter bounced through an open doorway. "Under different circumstances I'd introduce you to my family. But I'd rather not put them under any more stress."

"We'll leave them out of it."

"I wish that were possible." Saying nothing more, Mira started upstairs.

The house reflected her, Eve decided. Calming colors,

soft edges, perfect style. Her home office was half the size of her official one and must at one time have been a small bedroom. Eve noted that she'd furnished it with deep chairs and what she thought of as a lady's desk, with curved legs and fancy carving.

Mira adjusted the sunscreen on a window and turned to the mini AutoChef recessed into the wall.

"You'll have reviewed my original profile on David Palmer," she began, satisfied that her hands were steady as she programmed for tea. "I would stand by it, with a few additions due to his time in prison."

"I didn't come for a profile. I've got him figured."

"Do you?"

"I walked around inside his head before. We both did."

"Yes." Mira offered Eve a delicate cup filled with the fragrant tea they both knew she didn't want. "In some ways he remains the exception to a great many rules. He had a loving and advantaged childhood. Neither of his parents exhibits any signs of emotional or psychological defects. He did well in school, more of an overachiever than under-, but nothing off the scale. Testing showed no brain deformities, no physical abnormalities. There is no psychological or physiological root for his condition."

"He likes it," Eve said briefly. "Sometimes evil's its own root."

"I want to disagree," Mira murmured. "The reasons, the whys of abnormal behavior are important to me. But I have no reasons, no whys, for David Palmer."

"That's not your problem, Doctor. Mine is to stop him, and to protect the people he's chosen. The first two on his list are dead."

"Stephanie Ring? You're sure."

"Her body was found this morning. Carl Neissan's been taken."

This time Mira's hand shook, rattling her cup in its saucer before she set it aside. "He was under guard."

"Palmer got himself into a cop suit, knocked on the damn door, and posed as the relief. The on-duty didn't question it. He went home to a late Christmas dinner. When the morning duty came on, he found the house empty.''

"And the night relief? The real one?''

"Inside the trunk of his unit. Tranq'd and bound but otherwise unharmed. He hasn't come around enough to be questioned yet. Hardly matters. We know it was Palmer. I'm arranging for Justine Polinsky to be moved to a safe house. You'll want to pack some things, Doctor. You're going under.''

"You know I can't do that, Eve. This is as much my case as yours.''

"You're wrong. You're a consultant, and that's it. I don't need consultation. I'm no longer confident that you can be adequately protected in this location. I'm moving you.''

"Eve—''

"Don't fuck with me.'' It came out sharp, very close to mean, and Mira jerked back in surprise. "I'm taking you into police custody. You can gather up some personal things or you can go as you are. But you're going.''

Calling on the control that ran within her like her own bloodstream, Mira folded her hands in her lap. "And you? Will you be going under?''

"I'm not your concern.''

"Of course you are, Eve,'' Mira said quietly, watching the storm of emotions in Eve's eyes. "Just as I'm yours. And my family downstairs is mine. They're not safe.''

"I'll see to it. I'll see to them.''

Mira nodded, closed her eyes briefly. "It would be a great relief to me to know they were away from here, and protected. It's difficult for me to cope when I'm worried about their welfare.''

"He won't touch them. I promise you.''

"I'll take your word. Now as to my status—''

"I didn't give you multiple choices, Dr. Mira.''

"Just a moment.'' Composed again, Mira picked up her tea. "I think you'll agree . . . I have every bit as much influence with your superiors as you do. It would hardly serve either of us to play at tugging strings. I'm not being stubborn or courageous,'' she added. "Those are your traits.''

A ghost of a smile curved her mouth when Eve frowned at her. "I admire them. You're also a woman who can see past emotion to the goal. The goal is to stop David Palmer. I can be of use. We both know it. With my family away I'll be less distracted. And I can't be with them, Eve, because if I am I'll worry that he'll harm one of them to get to me."

She paused for a moment, judged that Eve was considering. "I have no argument to having guards here or at my office. In fact, I want them. Very much. I have no intention of taking any unnecessary chances or risks. I'm just asking you to let me do my work."

"You can do your work where I put you."

"Eve." Mira drew a breath. "If you put both me and Justine out of his reach, there's the very real possibility he'll take someone else." She nodded. "You've considered that already. He won't come for you until he's ready. You're the grand prize. If no one else is accessible, he'll strike out. He'll want to keep to his timetable, even if it requires a substitute."

"I've got some lines on him."

"And you'll find him. But if he believes I'm accessible, if I'm at least visible, he'll be satisfied to focus his energies on getting through. I expect you to prevent that." She smiled again, easier now. "And I intend to do everything I can to help you."

"I can make you go. All your influence won't matter if I toss you in restraints and have you hauled out of here. You'll be pissed off, but you'll be safe."

"I wouldn't put it past you," Mira agreed. "But you know I'm right."

"I'm doubling your guards. You're wearing a bracelet. You work here. You're not to leave the house for any reason." Her eyes flashed when Mira started to protest. "You push me on this, you're going to find out what it feels like to wear cuffs." Eve rose. "Your guards will do hourly check-ins. Your 'link will be monitored."

"That hardly makes me appear accessible."

"He'll know you're here. That's going to have to be

enough. I've got work to do." Eve started for the door, hesitated, then spoke without turning around. "Your family, they matter to you."

"Yes, of course."

"You matter to me." She walked away quickly, before Mira could get shakily to her feet.

SIX

Eve headed to the lab from Mira's. From there she planned a stop by the morgue and another at Carl Neissan's before returning to her home office.

Remembering Mira's concern about family, Eve called Roarke on her palm-link after she parked and started into the building.

"Why are you alone?" was the first thing he said to her.

"Cut it out." She flashed her badge at security, then headed across the lobby and down toward the labs. "I'm in a secured facility, surrounded by rent-a-cops, monitors, and lab dorks. I've got a job to do. Let me do it."

"He's gotten three out of six."

She stopped, rolled her eyes. "Oh, I get it. Shows what kind of faith you have in me. I guess being a cop for ten years makes me as easy a fish as a seventy-year-old judge and a couple of soft lawyers."

"You annoy me, Eve."

"Why? Because I'm right?"

"Yes. And snotty about it." But his smile warmed a little. "Why did you call?"

"So I could be snotty. I'm at the lab, about to tackle Dickhead. I've got a few stops to make after this. I'll check in."

It was a casual way to let him know she understood he worried. And he accepted, in the same tone. "I've several 'link conferences this afternoon. Call in on the private line. Watch your back, Lieutenant. I'm very fond of it."

Satisfied, she swung into the lab. Dickie, the chief tech, was there, looking sleepy-eyed and pale as he stared at the readout on his monitor.

The last time she'd been in the lab, there'd been a hell of a party going on. Now those who'd bothered to come in worked sluggishly and looked worse.

"I need reports, Dickie. Wainger and Ring."

"Jesus, Dallas." He looked up mournfully, hunching his shoulders. "Don't you ever stay home?"

Since he looked ill, she gave him a little leeway. Silently she opened her jacket, tapped the silver star pinned to her shirt. "I'm the law," she said soberly. "The law has no home."

It made him grin a little, then he moaned. "Man, I got the mother of all Christmas hangovers."

"Mix yourself up a potion, Dickie, and get over it. Dave's got number three."

"Dave who?"

"Palmer, David Palmer." She resisted letting out her impatience by cuffing him on the side of the head. But she imagined doing it. "Did you read the damn directive?"

"I've only been here twenty minutes. Jesus." He rolled his shoulders, rubbed his face, drew in three sharp nasal breaths. "Palmer? That freak's caged."

"Not anymore. He skipped and he's back in New York. Wainger and Ring are his."

"Shit. Damn shit." He didn't look any less ill, but his eyes were alert now. "Fucking Christmas week and we get the world's biggest psycho-freak."

"Yeah, and Happy New Year, too. I need the results, on the rope, on the paper. I want to know what he used to carve the letters. You get any hair or fiber from the sweepers?''

''No, wait, just wait a damn minute.'' He scooted his rolling chair down the counter, barked orders at a computer, muttering as he scanned the data. ''Bodies were clean. No hair other than victim's. No fiber.''

''He always kept them clean,'' Eve murmured.

''Yeah, I remember. I remember. Got some dust—like grit between the toes, both victims.''

''Concrete dust.''

''Yeah. Get you the grade, possible age. Now the rope.'' He skidded back. ''I was just looking at it, just doing the test run. Nothing special or exotic about it. Standard nylon strapping rope. Give me some time, I'll get you the make.''

''How much time?''

''Two hours, three tops. Takes longer when it's standard.''

''Make it fast.'' She swung away. ''I'm in the field.''

She stopped at the morgue next, to harass the chief medical examiner. It was more difficult to intimidate Morse or to rush him.

No sexual assault or molestation, no mutilation or injuries of genitalia.

Typical of Palmer, Eve thought as she ran over Morse's prelim report in her head. He was as highly asexual as anyone she'd come up against. She doubted that he even thought of the gender of his victims other than as a statistic for his experiments.

Subject Wainger's central nervous system had been severely damaged. Subject suffered minor cardiac infarction during abduction and torture period. Anus and interior of mouth showed electrical burns. Both hands crushed with a smooth, heavy instrument. Three ribs cracked.

The list of injuries went on until Morse had confirmed the cause of death as strangulation. And the time of death as midnight, December twenty-fourth.

She spent an hour at Carl Neissan's, another at Wainger's. In both cases, she thought, the door had been opened,

Palmer allowed in. He was good at that. Good at putting on a pretty smile and talking his way in.

He looked so damn innocent, Eve thought as she climbed the steps to her own front door. Even the eyes—and the eyes usually told you—were those of a young, harmless man. They hadn't flickered, hadn't glazed or brightened, even when he'd sat in interview across from her and described each and every murder.

They'd taken on the light of madness only when he talked about the scope and importance of his work.

"Lieutenant." Summerset, tall and bony in severe black, slipped out of a doorway. "Do I assume your guests will be remaining for lunch?"

"Guests? I don't have any guests." She stripped off her jacket, tossed it across the newel post. "If you mean my team, we'll deal with it."

He had the jacket off the post even as she started up the stairs. At his low growl of disgust she glanced back. He held in his fingertips the gloves she'd balled into her jacket pocket. "What have you done to these?"

"It's just sealant." Which she'd forgotten to clean off before she shoved them into her pocket.

"These are handmade, Italian leather with mink lining."

"Mink? Shit. What is he, crazy?" Shaking her head, she kept on going. "Mink lining, for Christ's sake. I'll have lost them by next week, then some stupid mink will have died for nothing." She glanced down the hallway at Roarke's office door, shook her head again, and walked into her own.

She was right, Eve noted. Her team could deal with lunch on their own. Feeney was chowing down on some kind of multitiered sandwich while he muttered orders into the computer and scanned. Peabody had a deep bowl of pasta, scooping it up one-handed, sliding printouts into a pile with the other.

Her office smelled like an upscale diner and sounded like cops. Computer and human voices clashed, the printer hummed, and the main 'link was beeping and being ignored.

She strode over and answered it herself. "Dallas."

"Hey, got your rope." When she saw Dickie shove a pickle in his mouth, she wondered if every city official's stomach had gone on alarm at the same time. "Nylon strapping cord, like I said. This particular type is top grade, heavy load. Manufactured by Kytell outta Jersey. You guys run the distributor, that's your end."

"Yeah. Thanks." She broke transmission, thinking Dickie wasn't always a complete dickhead. He'd come through and hadn't required a bribe.

"Lieutenant," Peabody began, but Eve held up a finger and walked to Roarke's door and through it. "Do you own Kytell in New Jersey?"

Then she stopped and winced when she saw that he was in the middle of a holographic conference. Several images turned, studied her out of politely annoyed eyes.

"Sorry."

"It's all right. Gentlemen, ladies, this is my wife." Roarke leaned back in his chair, monumentally amused that Eve had inadvertently made good on her threat to barge in on one of his multimillion-dollar deals just to annoy him. "If you'd excuse me one moment. Caro?"

The holo of his administrative assistant rose, smiled. "Of course. We'll shift to the boardroom momentarily." The image turned, ran her hands over controls that only she could see, and the holos winked away.

"I should have knocked or something."

"It's not a problem. They'll hold. I'm about to make them all very rich. Do I own what?"

"Did you have to say 'my wife' just that way, like I'd just run up from the kitchen?"

"So much more serene an image than telling them you'd just run in from the morgue. And it is a rather conservative company I'm about to buy. Now, do I own what and why do you want to know?"

"Kytell, based in New Jersey. They make rope."

"Do they? Well, I have no idea. Just a minute." He swiveled at the console, asked for the information on the company. Which, Eve thought with some irritation, she could have damn well done herself.

"Yes, they're an arm of Yancy, which is part of Roarke Industries. And which, I assume, made the murder weapon."

"Right the first time."

"Then you'll want the distributor, the stores in the New York area where large quantities were sold to one buyer within the last week."

"Peabody can get it."

"I'll get it faster. Give me thirty minutes to finish up in here, then I'll shoot the data through to your unit."

"Thanks." She started out, turned back. "The third woman on the right? The redhead? She was giving you a leg shot—another inch of skirt lift and it would have been past her crotch."

"I noticed. Very nice legs." He smiled. "But she still won't get more than eighty point three a share. Anything else?"

"She's no natural redhead," Eve said for the hell of it and heard him laugh as she shut the door between them.

"Sir." Peabody got to her feet. "I think I have a line on the vehicle. Three possibles, high-end privates sold to single men in their early to mid-twenties on December twentieth and twenty-first. Two dealerships on the East Side and one in Brooklyn."

"Print hard copies of Palmer's photo."

"Already done."

"Feeney?"

"Whittling it down."

"Keep whittling. Roarke should have some data on the murder weapon inside a half hour. Send what he has to me in the field, will you? Peabody, you're with me."

The first dealership was a wash, and as she pulled up at the second, Eve sincerely hoped she didn't have to head to Brooklyn. The shiny new vehicles on the showroom floor had Peabody's eyes gleaming avariciously. Only Eve's quick elbow jab kept her from stroking the hood of a

Booster-6Z, the sport-utility vehicle of the year.

"Maintain some dignity," Eve muttered. She flagged a salesman, who looked none too happy when she flipped out her badge. "I need to talk to the rep who sold a rig like this"—she gestured toward the Booster—"last week. Young guy bought it."

"Lana sold one of the 6Zs a few days before Christmas." Now he looked even unhappier. "She often rounds up the younger men." He pointed to a woman at a desk on the far side of the showroom.

"Thanks." Eve walked over, noting that Lana had an explosion of glossy black curls cascading down her back, a headset over it, and was fast-talking a potential customer on the line while she manually operated a keyboard with fingernails painted a vivid red.

"I can put you in it for eight a month. Eight a month and you're behind the wheel of the sexiest, most powerful land and air unit currently produced. I'm slicing my commission to the bone because I want to see you drive off in what makes you happy."

"Make him happy later, Lana." Eve held her badge in front of Lana's face.

Lana put a hand over the mouthpiece, studied the ID, cursed softly. Then her voice went back to melt. "Jerry, you take one more look at the video, try out the holo run. If you're not smiling by the end of it, the 7000's not the one for you. You call me back and let me know. Remember, I want you happy. Hear?"

She disconnected, glared at Eve. "I paid those damn parking violations. Every one."

"Glad to hear it. Our city needs your support. I need information on a sale you made last week. Booster. You were contacted earlier today and confirmed."

"Yeah, right. Nice guy, pretty face." She smiled. "He knew what he wanted right off."

"Is this the guy?" Eve signaled to Peabody, who took out the photo.

"Yeah. Cute."

"Yeah, he's real cute. I need the data. Name, address, the works."

"Sure, no problem." She turned to her machine, asked for the readout. Then, looking back up at Eve, she narrowed her eyes. "You look familiar. Have I sold you a car?"

Eve thought of her departmental issue, its sad pea-green finish and blocky style. "No."

"You really look— Oh!" Lana lit up like a Christmas tree. "Sure, sure, you're Roarke's wife. Roarke's cop wife. I've seen you on screen. Word is he's got an extensive collection of vehicles. Where does he deal?"

"Wherever he wants," Eve said shortly, and Lana let out a gay laugh.

"Oh, I'm sure he does. I'd absolutely love to show him our brand-new Barbarian. It won't be on the market for another three months, but I can arrange a private showing. If you'd just give him my card, Mrs. Roarke, I'll be—"

"You see this?" Eve took out her badge again, all but pushed it into Lana's pert nose. "It says 'Dallas.' Lieutenant Dallas. I'm not here to liaison your next commission. This is an official investigation. Give me the damn data."

"Certainly. Of course." If her feathers were ruffled, Lana hid it well. "Um, the name is Peter Nolan, 123 East Sixty-eighth, apartment 4-B."

"How'd he pay?"

"That I remember. Straight E-transfer. The whole shot. Didn't want to finance. The transfer was ordered, received, and confirmed, and he drove off a happy man."

"I need all the vehicle information, including temp license and registration number. Full description."

"All right. Gee, what'd he do? Kill somebody?"

"Yeah, he did."

"Wow." Lana busily copied the data disc. "You just can't trust a pretty face," she said and slipped her business card into the disc pack.

SEVEN

Peter Nolan didn't live at the Sixty-eighth Street address. The Kowaskis, an elderly couple, and their creaky schnauzer had lived there for fifteen years.

A check of the bank showed that the Nolan account had been opened, in person, on December 20 of that year and closed on December 22.

Just long enough to do the deal, Eve thought. But where had he gotten the money?

Taking Roarke's advice, she rounded out a very long day by starting searches on accounts under the name of Palmer. It would, she thought, rubbing her eyes, take a big slice of time.

How much time did Carl have? she wondered. Another day, by her guess. If Palmer was running true to form, he would begin to enjoy his work too much to rush through it. But sometime within the next twenty-four hours, she believed he'd try for Justine Polinsky.

While her machine worked, she leaned back and closed her eyes. Nearly midnight, she thought. Another day. Feeney was working his end. She was confident they'd have a

line on the equipment soon, then there were the houses to
check. They had the make, model, and license of his vehicle.

He'd left a trail, she thought. He wanted her to follow
it, wanted her close. The son of a bitch.

It's you and me, isn't it, Dave? she thought as her mind
started to drift. How fast can I be, and how clever? You
figure it'll make it all the sweeter when you've got me in
that cage. It's because you want that so bad that you're
making mistakes. Little mistakes.

I'm going to hang you with them.

She slid into sleep while her computer hummed and
woke only when she felt herself being lifted.

"What?" Reflexively she reached for the weapon she'd
already unharnessed.

"You need to be in bed." Roarke held her close as he
left the office.

"I was just resting my eyes. I've got data coming in.
Don't carry me."

"You were dead out, the data will be there in the morning, and I'm already carrying you."

"I'm getting closer, but not close enough."

He'd seen the financial data on her screen. "I'll take a
look through the accounts in the morning," he told her as
he laid her on the bed.

"I've got it covered."

He unpinned her badge, set it aside. "Yes, Sheriff, but
money is my business. Close it down a while."

"He'll be sleeping now." She let Roarke undress her.
"In a big, soft bed with clean sheets. Dave likes to be clean
and comfortable. He'll have a monitor in the bedroom so
he can watch Neissan. He likes to watch before he goes to
sleep. He told me."

"Don't think." Roarke slipped into bed beside her, gathered her close.

"He wants me."

"Yes, I know." Roarke pressed his lips to her hair as
much to comfort himself as her. "But he can't have you."

•   •   •

Sleep helped. She'd dropped into it like a stone and had lain on the bottom of the dreaming pool for six hours. There'd been no call in the middle of the night to tell her Carl Neissan's body had been found.

Another day, she thought again and strode into her office. Roarke was at her desk, busily screening data.

"What are you doing?" She all but leapt to him. "That's classified."

"Don't pick nits, darling. You were going too broad last night. You'll be days compiling and rejecting all accounts under the name Palmer. You want one that shows considerable activity, large transfers, and connections to other accounts—which is, of course, the trickier part if you're dealing with someone who understands how to hide the coin."

"You can't just sit down and start going through data accumulated in an investigation."

"Of course I can. You need coffee." He looked up briefly. "Then you'll feel more yourself and I'll show you what I have."

"I feel exactly like myself." Which, she admitted, at the moment was annoyed and edgy. She stalked to the AutoChef in the kitchen, went for an oversized mug of hot and black. The rich and real caffeine Roarke could command zipped straight through her system.

"What have you got?" she demanded when she walked back in.

"Palmer was too simple, too obvious," Roarke began, and she narrowed her eyes.

"You didn't think so yesterday."

"I said check for relatives, same names. I should have suggested you try his mother's maiden name. Riley. And here we have the account of one Palmer Riley. It was opened six years ago, standard brokerage account, managed. Since there's been some activity over the last six months, I would assume your man found a way to access a 'link or computer from prison."

"He shouldn't have been near one. How can you be sure?"

"He understands how money works, and just how fluid it can be. You see here that six months ago he had a balance of just over $1.3 million. For the past three years previous, all action was automatic, straight managed with no input from the account holder. But here he begins to make transfers. Here's one to an account under Peter Nolan, which, by the way, is his aunt's husband's name on his father's side. Overseas accounts, off-planet accounts, local New York accounts—different names, different IDs. He's had this money for some time and he waited, sat on it until he found the way to use it."

"When I took him down before, we froze his accounts, accounts under David Palmer. We didn't look deeper. I didn't think of it."

"Why should you have? You stopped him, you put him away. He was meant to stay away."

"If I'd cleared it all, he wouldn't have had the backing to come back here."

"Eve, he'd have found a way." He waited until she looked at him. "You know that."

"Yeah." She let out a long breath. "Yeah, I know that. This tells me he's been planning, he's been shopping, he's been juggling funds, funneling into cover accounts. I need to freeze them. I don't think a judge is going to argue with me, not after what happened to one of their own."

"You'll piss him off."

"That's the plan. I need the names, numbers, locations of all the accounts you can connect to him." She blew out a breath. "Then I guess I owe you."

"Use your present, and we'll call it even."

"My present? Oh, yeah. Where and/or when do I want to go for a day. Let me mull that over a little bit. We get this wrapped, I'll use it for New Year's Eve."

"There's a deal."

A horrible thought snuck into her busy mind. "We don't have like a thing for New Year's, do we? No party or anything."

"No. I didn't want anything but you."

She looked back at him, narrowing her eyes even as the

smile spread. "Do you practice saying stuff like that?"

"No." He rose, framed her face and kissed her, hard and deep. "I have all that stuff on disc."

"You're a slick guy, Roarke." She skimmed her fingers through her hair and simply lost herself for a moment in the look of him. Then, giving herself a shake, she stepped back. "I have to work."

"Wait." He grabbed her hand before she could turn away. "What was that?"

"I don't know. It just comes over me sometimes. You, I guess, come over me sometimes. I don't have time for it now."

"Darling Eve." He brushed his thumb over her knuckles. "Be sure to make time later."

"Yeah, I'll do that."

They worked together for an hour before Peabody arrived. She switched gears, leaving Roarke to do what he did best—manipulate data—while she focused on private residences purchased in the New York area, widening the timing to the six months since Palmer had activated his account.

Feeney called in to let her know he'd identified some of the equipment from the recording and was following up.

Eve gathered her printouts and rose. "We've got more than thirty houses to check. Have to do it door-to-door since I don't trust the names and data. He could have used anything. Peabody—"

"I'm with you, sir."

"Right. Roarke, I'll be in the field."

"I'll let you know when I have this wrapped."

She looked at him, working smoothly, thoroughly, methodically. And wondered who the hell was dealing with what she often thought of as his empire. "Look, I can call a man in for this. McNab—"

"McNab." Peabody winced at the name before she could stop herself. She had a temporary truce going with the EDD detective, but that didn't mean she wanted to share her case with him. Again. "Dallas, come on. It's been so nice and quiet around here."

"I've got this." Roarke shot her a glance, winked at Peabody. "I have an investment in it now."

"Whatever. Shoot me, and Feeney, the data when you have it all. I'm going to check out the rope, too. He likely picked up everything himself, but it would only take one delivery to pin down his hole."

After three hours of knocking on doors, questioning professional parents, housekeepers, or others who chose the work-at-home route, Eve took pity on Peabody and swung by a glide cart.

In this neighborhood the carts were clean, the awnings or umbrellas bright, the operators polite. And the prices obscene.

Peabody winced as she was forced to use a credit card for nothing but coffee, a kabob, and a small scoop of paper-thin oil chips.

"It's my metabolism," she muttered as she climbed back into the car. "I have one that requires fuel at regular intervals."

"Then pump up," Eve advised. "It's going to be a long day. At least half these people aren't going to be home until after the five o'clock shift ends."

She snagged the 'link when it beeped. "Dallas."

"Hello, Lieutenant." Roarke eyed her soberly. "Your data's coming through."

"Thanks. I'll start on the warrant."

"One thing—I didn't find any account with a withdrawal or transfer that seemed large enough for a purchase or down payment on a house. A couple are possible, but if, as you told me, he didn't finance a car, it's likely he didn't want to deal with the credit and Compuguard checks on his rating and background."

"He's got a damn house, Roarke. I know it."

"I'm sure you're right. I'm not convinced he acquired it recently."

"I've still got twenty-couple to check," she replied. "I

have to follow through on that. Maybe he's just renting. He likes to own, but maybe this time he's renting. I'll run it through that way, too.''

''There weren't any standard transfers or withdrawals that would indicate rent or mortgage payments.''

She hissed out a breath. ''It's ridiculous.''

''What?''

''How good a cop you'd make.''

''I don't think insulting me is appropriate under the circumstances. I have some business of my own to tend to,'' he said when she grinned at him. ''I'll get back to yours shortly.''

Palmer had purchased, and personally picked up, a hundred twenty yards of nylon rope from a supply warehouse store off Canal. The clerk who had handled the sale ID'd the photo and mentioned what a nice young man Mr. Dickson had been. As Dickson, Palmer had also purchased a dozen heavy-load pulleys, a supply of steel O rings, cable, and the complete Handy Homemaker set of Steelguard tools, including the accessory laser package.

The entire business had been loaded into the cargo area of his shiny new Booster-6Z—which the clerk had admired—on the morning of December 22.

Eve imagined Palmer had been a busy little bee that day and throughout the next, setting up his private chamber of horrors.

By eight they'd eliminated all the houses on Eve's initial list.

''That's it.'' Eve climbed back in her vehicle and pressed her fingers to her eyes. ''They all check out. I'll drop you at a transpo stop, Peabody.''

''Are you going home?''

Eve lowered her hands. ''Why?''

''Because I'm not going off duty if you're starting on the list of rentals I ran.''

''Excuse me?''

Peabody firmed her chin. Eve could arrow a cold chill up your spine when she took on that superior-officer tone.

"I'm not going off duty, sir, to leave you solo in the field with Palmer on the loose and you as a target. With respect, Lieutenant."

"You don't think I can handle some little pissant, mentally defective?"

"I think you want to handle him too much." Peabody sucked in a breath. "I'm sticking, Dallas."

Eve narrowed her eyes. "Have you been talking to Roarke?" At the quick flicker in Peabody's eyes Eve swore. "Goddamn it."

"He's right and you're wrong. Sir." Peabody braced for the explosion, was determined to weather it, then all but goggled with shock.

"Maybe," was all Eve said as she pulled away from the curb.

Since she was on a roll, Peabody slanted Eve a look. "You haven't eaten all day. You didn't even steal any of my oil chips. You could use a meal."

"Okay, okay. Christ, Roarke's got your number, doesn't he?"

"I wish."

"Zip it, Peabody. We'll fuel the metabolism, then start on the rental units."

"Zipping with pleasure, sir."

EIGHT

It began to snow near midnight, fat, cold flakes with icy edges. Eve watched it through the windshield and told herself it was time to stop. The night was over. Nothing more could be done.

"He's got all the cards," she murmured.

"You've got a pretty good hand, Dallas." Peabody shifted in her seat, grateful for the heat of the car. Even her bones were chilled.

"Doesn't matter what I've got." Eve drove away from the last rental unit they'd checked. "Not tonight. I know who he is, who he's going to kill. I know how he does it and I know why. And tonight it doesn't mean a damn thing. Odds are, he's done with Carl now."

It was rare to see Eve discouraged. Angry, yes, Peabody thought with some concern. And driven. But she couldn't recall ever hearing that quiet resignation in her lieutenant's voice before. "You covered all the angles. You took all the steps."

"That's not going to mean much to Carl. And if I'd covered all the angles, I'd have the son of a bitch. So I'm missing one. He's slipping through because I can't pin it.''

"You've only had the case for three days."

"No. I've had it for three years." As she pulled up at a light, her 'link beeped. "Dallas."

"Lieutenant, this is Detective Dalrymple, assigned to observation on the Polinsky residence. We've got a mixed-race male, mid-twenties, average height and build. Subject is on foot and carrying a small sack. He used what appeared to be a key code to gain access to premises. He's inside now."

"I'm three blocks east of your location and on my way." She'd already whipped around the corner. "Secure all exists, call for backup. Doesn't make sense," she muttered to Peabody as they barreled across Madison. "Right out in the open? Falls right into our laps? Doesn't fucking make sense."

She squealed to a stop a half a block from the address. Her weapon was in her hand before she hit the sidewalk. "Peabody, the Polinsky unit is on four, south side. Go around, take the fire escape. He comes out that way, take him down quick."

Eve charged in at the front of the building and, too impatient for the elevator, raced up the stairs. She found Dalrymple on four, weapon drawn as he waited beside the door.

"Lieutenant." He gave her a brief nod. "My partner's around the back. Subject's been inside less than five minutes. Backup's on the way."

"Good." She studied Dalrymple's face, found his eyes steady. "We won't wait for them. I go in low," she added, taking out her master and bypassing the locks.

"Fine with me." He was ready beside her.

"On three. One, two." They hit the door, went through high and low, back to back, sweeping with their weapons. Music was playing, a primitive backbeat of drums behind screaming guitars. In the tidy living area, the mood screen had been set on deep reds and swimming blues melting into each other.

She signaled Dalrymple to the left, had taken two steps

to the right herself when a naked man came out of the kitchen area carrying a bottle of wine and a single red rose.

He screamed and dropped the bottle. Wine glugged out onto the rug. Holding the rose to his balls, he crouched. "Don't shoot! Jesus, don't shoot. Take anything you want. Anything. It's not even mine."

"NYPSD," Eve snapped at him. "On the floor, face-down, hands behind your head. Now!"

"Yes, ma'am, yes, ma'am." He all but dove to the rug. "I didn't do anything." He flinched when Eve dragged his hands down and cuffed them. "I was just going to meet Sunny. She said it would be okay."

"Who the hell are you?"

"Jimmy. Jimmy Ripsky. I go to college with Sunny. We're on winter break. She said her parents were out of town for a few days and we could use the place."

Eve holstered her weapon in disgust. The boy was shaking like a leaf. "Get him a blanket or something, Dalrymple. This isn't our man." She dragged him to his feet and had enough pity in her to uncuff him before gesturing to a chair. "Let's here the whole story, Jimmy."

"That's it. Um"—cringing with embarrassment, he folded his arms over his crotch—"Sunny and I are, like, an item."

"And who's Sunny?"

"Sunny Polinsky. Sheila, I guess. Everybody calls her Sunny. This is her parents' place. Man, her father's going to kill me if he finds out."

"She called you?"

"Yeah. Well, no." He looked up with desperate gratitude when Dalrymple came in with a chenille throw. "I got an E-mail from her this morning and a package. She said her parents were going south for the week and how I should come over tonight. About midnight, let myself in with the key she'd sent me. And I should, um, you know, get comfortable." He tucked the throw more securely around his legs. "She said she'd be here by twelve-thirty and I should, well, ah, be waiting in bed." He moistened his lips. "It was pretty, sort of, explicit for Sunny."

"Do you still have the E-mail? The package the key came in?"

"I dumped the package in the recycler, but I've got the E-mail. I printed it out. It's . . . it's a keeper, you know?"

"Right. Detective, call in your partner and my aide."

"Um, ma'am?" Jimmy began when Dalrymple turned away with his communicator.

"Dallas. Lieutenant."

"Yes, ma'am, Lieutenant. What's going on? Is Sunny okay?"

"She's fine. She's with her parents."

"But—she said she'd be here."

"I think someone else sent you that keeper E-mail. Somebody who wanted me to have a little something extra to do tonight." But she sat, pulled out her palm-link. "I'm going to check out your story, Jimmy. If it all fits, Detective Dalrymple's going to arrange for a uniform to take you home. You can give him the printout of the E-mail—and your computer."

"My computer? But—"

"It's police business," she said shortly. "You'll get it back."

"Well, that was fun," Peabody said when Eve resecured the door.

"A barrel of laughs."

"Poor kid. He was mortified. Here he was thinking he was going to have the sex of his dreams with his girl, and he gets busted."

"The fact that a rosebud managed to preserve most of his modesty tells me that the sex of his dreams outruns the reality." At Peabody's snort, Eve turned to the elevator. "Sunny backed up his story about them being an item. Not that I doubted it. The kid was too scared to lie. So . . . Dave's been keeping up with the social activities of his marks. He knows the family, the friends, and he knows how to use them."

She stepped out of the elevator, crossed the lobby. "For an MD in a maximum lockup, he managed to get his hands on plenty of data."

She paused at the door and simply stood for a moment looking out at the thin, steady snow. "You got off-planet clearance, Peabody?"

"Sure. It's a job requirement."

"Right. Well, go home and pack a bag. I want you on your way to Rexal on the first transport we can arrange. You and McNab can check out the facilities, find the unit Palmer had access to."

The initial rush from the idea of an off-planet assignment turned to ashes in her mouth. "McNab? I don't need McNab."

"When you find the unit, you'll need a good electronics man." Eve opened the door, and the blast of cold cooled the annoyed flush on Peabody's cheeks.

"He's a pain in the ass."

"Sure he is, but he knows his job. If Feeney can spare him, you're the off-planet team." She reached for her communicator, intending to interrupt Feeney's sleep and get the ball rolling. A scream from the end of the block had her drawing her weapon instead.

She pounded west, boots digging into the slick sidewalk. With one quick gesture, she signaled Dalrymple to stay at his post in the surveillance van.

She saw the woman first, wrapped in sleek black fur, clinging to a man with an overcoat over a tux. He was trying to shield her face and muffle her mouth against his shoulder. The pitch and volume of her screams indicated he wasn't doing a very good job of it.

"Police!" He shouted it as he saw Peabody and Eve running toward them. "Here's the police, honey. My God, my God, what's this city coming to? He threw it out, threw it out right at our feet."

It, Eve saw, was Carl Neissan. His naked and broken body lay face up against the curb. His head had been shaved, she noted, and the tender skin abraded and burned. His knees were shattered, his protruding tongue blackened. Around his neck, digging deep, was the signature noose. And the message carved into his chest was still red and raw.

WOE UNTO YOU ALSO, YE LAWYERS!

The woman's screaming had turned to wailing now. Eve tuned it out. With her eyes on the body, she pulled out her communicator. "This is Dallas, Lieutenant Eve. I have a homicide."

She gave Dispatch the necessary information, then turned to the male witness. "You live around here?"

"Yes, yes, this building on the corner. We were just coming home from a party when—"

"My aide is going to take your companion inside, away from this. Out of the cold. We'll need her statement. I'd appreciate it if you'd stay out here with me for a few minutes."

"Yes, of course. Yes. Honey." He tried to pry his wife's hands from around his neck. "Honey, you go with the policewoman. Go inside now."

"Peabody," Eve said under her breath, "take honey out of here, get what you can out of her."

"Yes, sir. Ma'am, come with me." With a couple of firm tugs Peabody had the woman.

"It was such a shock," he continued. "She's very delicate, my wife. It's such a shock."

"Yes, sir, I'm sure it is. Can I have your names, please?"

"What? Oh. Fitzgerald. George and Maria."

Eve got the names and the address on record. In a few minutes she would have a crowd to deal with, she knew. Even jaded New Yorkers would gather around a dead, naked body on Madison Avenue.

"Can you—sir, look at me," she added when he continued to stare at the body. He was going faintly green. "Look at me," she repeated, "and try to tell me exactly what happened."

"It was all so fast, so shocking." Reaction began to set in, showing in the way his hand trembled as he pressed it to his face. "We'd just come from the Andersons'. They had a holiday party tonight. It's only a block over, so we walked. We'd just crossed the street when there was a squeal of brakes. I barely paid attention to it—you know how it is."

"Yes, sir. What did you see?"

"I glanced back, just out of reflex, I suppose. I saw a dark car—black, I think. No, no, not a car—one of those utility vehicles. The sporty ones. It stopped right here. Right here. You can still see the skid marks in the snow. And then the door opened. He pushed—he all but flung this poor man out, right at our feet."

"You saw the driver?"

"Yes, yes, quite clearly. This corner is very well lit. He was a young man, handsome. Light hair. He smiled . . . he smiled at me just as the door opened. Why, I think I smiled back. He had the kind of face that makes you smile. I'm sure I could identify him. I'm sure of it."

"Yeah." Eve let out a breath, watched the wind snatch it away as the first black-and-whites arrived on the scene. You wanted to be seen, didn't you, Dave? she thought. And you wanted me to be close, very close, when you gave me Carl.

"You can go inside with your wife, Mr. Fitzgerald. I'll be in touch."

"Yes, of course. Thank you. I—it's Christmas week," he said with honest puzzlement in his eyes. "You live in the city, you know terrible things can and do happen. But it's Christmas week."

"Joy to the world," Eve murmured as he walked away. She turned around and ordered the uniforms to secure the scene and prepare for the crime-scene team. Then she crouched beside Carl and got to work.

NINE

Eve spent most of the next thirty hours backtracking, searching for the step she was sure she had missed. With Peabody off-planet, she did the work herself, rerunning searches and scans, compiling data, studying reports.

She did personal drop-bys at both the safe house where Justine and her family were being kept and Mira's home. She ran checks on their security bracelets to confirm that they were in perfect working order.

He couldn't get to them, she assured herself as she paced her office. With them out of reach, he would have no choice but to come for her.

Jesus, she wanted him to come for her.

It was a mistake, she knew it was a mistake, to make it a personal battle. But she could see his face too clearly, hear his soft prep-school voice so perfectly.

But you see, Lieutenant Dallas, the work you do is nothing more than a stopgap. You don't change anything. However many criminals you lock up today, there'll be that many and more tomorrow. What I'm doing changes everything. The answers to questions every human being asks.

How much is too much, how much will the mind accept, tolerate, bear, if you will, before it shuts down? And before it does, what thoughts, what impulses go through the mind as the body dies?

Death, Lieutenant, is the focus of your work and of mine. And while we both enjoy the brutality that goes with it, in the end I'll have my answers. You'll only have more questions.

She only had one question now, Eve thought. Where are you, Dave?

She turned back to her computer. "Engage, open file Palmer, H3492-G. Cross-reference all files and data pertaining to David Palmer. Run probability scan. What is the probability that Palmer, David, is now residing in New York City?"

Working. . . . Using current data the probability is ninety-seven point six that subject Palmer now resides in New York City.

"What is the probability that subject Palmer resides in a private home?"

Working. . . . probability ninety-five point eight that subject Palmer is residing in a private home at this time.

"Given the status of the three remaining targets of subject Palmer, which individual will he attempt to abduct next?"

Working. . . . strongest probability is for target Dallas, Lieutenant Eve. Attempts on targets Polinsky and Mira are illogical given current status.

"That's what you're hoping for."

She turned her head. Roarke stood in the doorway between their offices, watching her. "That's what I'm counting on."

"Why aren't you wearing a tracer bracelet?"

"They don't have one that goes with my outfit." She straightened, turned to face him. "I know what I'm doing."

"Do you?" He crossed to her. "Or are you too close to this one? He's gotten to you, Eve. He's upset your sense of balance. It's become almost intimate between you."

"It's always intimate."

"Maybe." He brushed a thumb just above her left cheekbone. Her eyes were shadowed, her face pale. She was, he knew, running on nerves and determination now. He'd seen it before. "In any case, you've interrupted his work. He has no one now."

"He won't wait long. I don't need the computer analysis to tell me that. We've got less than forty hours left in the year. I don't want to start the new one knowing he's out there. He won't want to start it without me."

"Neither do I."

"You won't have to." Because she sensed he needed it, she leaned into him, closed her mouth over his. "We've got a date."

"I'll hold you to it."

When she started to ease back, he slid his arms around her, brought her close. "I'm not quite done here," he murmured, and sent her blood swimming with a hard and hungry kiss.

For a moment that was all there was. The taste of him, the feel of him pressed against her, the need they created in each other time after time erupting inside her.

Giving herself to it, and to him, was as natural as breathing.

"Roarke, remember how on Christmas Eve we got naked and crazy?"

"Mmm." He moved his mouth to her ear, felt her tremble. "I believe I recall something of that."

"Well, prepare yourself for a review on New Year's Eve." She drew his head back, framing his face as she smiled at him. "I've decided it's one of our holiday traditions."

"I feel very warmly toward tradition."

"Yeah, and if I feel much warmer right now, I'm not going to get my job done, so . . ."

She jumped away from him when her 'link beeped and all but pounced on it. "Dallas."

"Lieutenant." Peabody's face swam on, swam off again, then came shakily back.

"Peabody, either your transmission's poor or you've grown a second nose."

"The equipment here's worse than what we deal with at Central." The audio came through with a snake hiss of static. "And I don't even want to talk about the food. When you're planning your next holiday vacation, steer clear of Rexal."

"And it was top of my list. What have you got for me?"

"I think we just caught a break. We've tracked down at least one unit Palmer had access to. It's in the chapel. He convinced the padre he'd found God and wanted to read Scripture and write an inspirational book on salvation."

"Glory hallelujah. Can McNab access his files?"

"He says he can. Shut up, McNab." Peabody turned her head. The fact that her face became a vivid orange could have been temper or space interference. "I'm giving this report. And I'm reporting, sir, that Detective McNab is still one big butt ache."

"So noted. What does he have so far?"

"He found the files on the book Palmer used to hose the preacher. And he *claims* he's working down the levels. Hey!"

The buzzing increased and the screen blurred with color, lines, figures. Eve pressed her fingers to her eyes and prayed for patience.

McNab's cheerful, attractive face came on. Eve noted that he wore six tiny silver hoops in one ear. So he hadn't decided to tone down his look for a visit to a rehabilitation center.

"Dallas. This guy knows his electronics, so he took basic precautions with his personal data, but—take a hike, She-Body, this is my area. Anyway, Lieutenant, I'm scraping off the excess now. He's got stuff tucked under his praise-the-Lord hype. It won't take me long to start picking it out. The trouble, other than your aide's constant griping, is transmitting to you. We've got crap equipment here and a meteor storm or some such happy shit happening. It's going to cause some problems."

"Can you work on the unit on a transport?"

"Ah . . . sure. Why not?"

"Confiscate the unit, catch the first transpo back. Report en route."

"Wow, that's iced. Confiscate. You hear that, She-Body? We're confiscating this little bastard."

"Get started," Eve ordered. "If they give you any grief, have the warden contact me. Dallas out."

Eve drove into Cop Central, making three unnecessary stops on the way. If Palmer was going to make a move on her, he'd do it on the street. He'd know he would never be able to break through the defenses of Roarke's fortress. But she spotted no tail, no shadow.

More, she didn't feel him.

Would he go for her in the station? she wondered as she took the glide up to the EDD sector to consult with Feeney. He'd used a cop's disguise to get to Carl. He could put it to use again, slip into the warrenlike building, blend with the uniforms.

It would be a risk, but a risk like that would increase the excitement, the satisfaction.

She studied faces as she went. Up glides, through breezeways, down corridors, past cubes and offices.

Once she'd updated Feeney and arranged for him to consult with McNab on the unit en route, she elbowed her way onto a packed elevator to make the trip to Commander Whitney's office.

She spent the morning moving through the building, inviting a confrontation, then she took to the streets for the afternoon.

She recanvased the houses she and Peabody had already hit. Left herself in the open. She bought bad coffee from a glide cart, loitered in the cold and the smoke of grilling soydogs.

What the hell was he waiting for? she thought in disgust, tossing the coffee cup into a recycling bin. The sound of a revving engine had her glancing over her shoulder. And she looked directly into Palmer's eyes.

He sat in his vehicle, grinned at her, blew her an exaggerated kiss. Even as she leaped forward, he hit vertical lift, shot up and streaked south.

She jumped into her car, going air as she squealed away from the curb. "Dispatch, Dallas, Lieutenant Eve. All units, all units in the vicinity of Park and Eighty respond. I'm in ground-to-air chase with murder suspect. Vehicle is a black new-issue Booster-6Z, New York license number Delta Able Zero-4821, temporary. Heading south on Park."

"Dispatch, Dallas. Received and confirmed. Units dispatched. Is subject vehicle in visual range?"

"No. Subject vehicle went air at Park and Eighty, headed south at high speed. Subject should be considered armed and dangerous."

"Acknowledged."

"Where'd you go, where'd you go, you little son of a bitch?" Eve rapped the wheel with her fist as she zipped down Park, shot down cross streets, circled back. "Too fast," she muttered. "You went under too fast. Your hole's got to be close."

She set down, did her best to bank her temper, to use her head and not her emotions. She'd let the search run another thirty minutes, though she'd already decided it was useless. He'd had the vehicle tucked away in a garage or lot minutes after she'd spotted him. After he'd made certain she'd spotted him.

That meant canvases of every parking facility in three sectors. Public and private. And with the budget, it would take days. The department wouldn't spare the manpower necessary to handle the job any quicker.

She stayed parked where she was, on the off chance that Palmer would try another taunt. After aborting the search, she did slow sweeps through the sectors herself, working off frustration before she drove home through the dark and the snarling traffic.

She didn't bother to snipe at Summerset, though he gave her ample opportunity. Instead, scooping up the cat, which circled her legs, she climbed the stairs. Her intent was to take a blistering-hot shower, drink a gallon of coffee, and go back to work.

Her reality was to fall facedown on the bed. Galahad climbed onto her butt, kneaded his way to comfort, curled up, and went on guard with his eyes slitted on the door.

That's how Roarke found them an hour later.

"I'll take over from here," he murmured, giving the cat a quick scratch between the ears. But when he started to drape a blanket over his wife, Eve stirred.

"I'm awake. I'm just—"

"Resting your eyes. Yes, I know." To keep her prone, Roarke stretched out beside her, stroked the hair away from her cheek. "Rest them a bit longer."

"I saw him today. The son of a bitch was ten feet away, and I lost him." She closed her eyes again. "He wants to piss me off so I stop thinking. Maybe I did, but I'm thinking now."

"And what are you thinking, Lieutenant?"

"That I've been counting too much on the fact that I know him, that I've been inside his head. I've been tracking him without factoring in one vital element."

"Which is?"

She opened her eyes again. "He's fucking crazy." She rolled over, stared at the sky window and the dark beyond it. "You can't predict insanity. Whatever the head shrinkers call it, it comes down to crazy. There's no physical, no psychological reason for it. It just is. He just is. I've been trying to predict the unpredictable. So I keep missing. It's not his work this time. It's payback. The other names on the list are incidental. It's me. He needed them to get to me."

"You'd already concluded that."

"Yeah, but what I didn't conclude, and what I'm concluding now, is he's willing to die, as long as he takes me out. He doesn't intend to go back to prison. I saw his eyes today. They were already dead."

"Which only makes him more dangerous."

"He has to find a way to get to me, so he'll take risks. But he won't risk going down before he's finished with me. He needs bait. Good bait. He must know about you."

She sat up now, raking her hair back. "I want you to wear a bracelet."

He lifted a brow. "I will if you will."

A muscle in her cheek jumped as she set her teeth. "I phrased that incorrectly. You're *going* to wear a bracelet."

"I believe such things are voluntary unless the subject has committed a crime." He sat up himself, caught her chin in his hand. "He won't get to you through me. That I can promise. But if you expect me to wear NYPSD accessories, you'll have to wear a matching one. Since you won't, I don't believe this conversation has a point."

"Goddamn it, Roarke. I can slap you into protective custody. I can order taps on all your communications, have you shadowed—"

"No," he interrupted, and infuriated her by kissing her lightly. "You can't. My lawyers will tap-dance all over your warrants. Stop." He tightened his grip on her chin before she could curse him again. And this time there was no light kiss, no flicker of amusement in his eyes. "You leave here every day to do a job that puts you in constant physical jeopardy. I don't ask you to change that. It's one of the reasons I fell in love with you. Who you are, what you do, why you do it. I don't ask you to change," he repeated. "Don't you ask me."

"It's just a precaution."

"No, it's a capitulation. If it was less, you'd be wearing one yourself."

She opened her mouth, shut it again, then shoved away and rose. "I hate when you're right. I really hate it. I'm going to take a shower. And don't even think about joining me and trying anything because I'm not too happy with you right now."

He merely reached out, snagged her hand, and yanked her back onto the bed. "I dare you to say that again in five minutes," he challenged and rolled on top of her.

She didn't say anything in five minutes, could barely speak in thirty. And when she did finally make it to the shower, her blood was still buzzing. She decided it was wiser not to comment when he joined her there. It would only appeal to his competitive streak.

She kept her silence and stepped out of the shower and into the drying tube. It gave her a very nice view. She let herself relax enough to enjoy it, watching the jets of water pulse and pound over Roarke as the hot air swirled around her.

She was back in the bedroom, just tugging on an ancient NYPSD sweatshirt and thinking about coffee and a long evening of work when her palm-link rang. Vaguely irritated with a call on her personal, she plucked it up from where she'd dumped it on the bedside table.

"Dallas."

"It was nice to see you today. In person. Face-to-face."

"Hello, Dave." With her free hand, she reached in her pocket, switched her communicator on, and plugged in Feeney's code. "Nice vehicle."

"Yes, I like it very much. Fast, efficient, spacious. You're looking a bit tired, Lieutenant. A bit pale. Overworked, as usual? Too bad you haven't been able to enjoy the holidays."

"They've had their moments."

"Mine have been very rewarding." His handsome face glowed with a smile. "It's so good to be back at work. Though I did manage to keep my hand in while I was away. But you and I—I'm sure we'll agree—know there's nothing like New York. Nothing like being home and doing what we love best."

"Too bad you won't be able to stay long."

"Oh, I intend to be here long enough to see the celebration in Times Square tomorrow night. To ring in the new year. In fact, I'm hoping we'll watch it together."

"Sorry, Dave. I have plans." From the corner of her eye, she watched Roarke come out of the bath. Watched him keep out of range, move directly to the bedroom computer, and begin to work manually.

"I think you'll change them. When you know who else I've invited to the party. I picked her up just a little while ago. You should be getting a call shortly from the guards you'd posted. The police haven't gotten any smarter since I've been gone.'' He let out a charming laugh. ''I took a little video for you, Dallas. Take a look. I'll be in touch later to tell you what you need to do to keep her alive.''

The image shifted. Eve's blood iced as she saw the woman in the cage. Unconscious, pale, one slim hand dangling through the bars.

''Transmitted from a public 'link,'' Roarke said from behind her. ''Grand Central.''

Dimly she heard Feeney giving her the same information through her communicator. Units were already on their way to the location.

He'd be gone. Of course they knew he'd already be gone.

''He has Mira.'' It was all she could say. ''He has Mira.''

TEN

Panic wanted to win. It crawled in her belly, snaked up her throat. It made her hands shake until she balled them into fists.

It wanted to swallow her when she moved through Mira's house, when she found the broken security bracelet on the floor of the office.

"He used laser tools." Her voice was steady and cool as she bagged the bracelet. "He anticipated that she'd be wearing one and brought what was necessary to remove it."

"The MTs are taking the guards in. The two from outside were just stunned. But one of the inside team's in bad shape." Feeney crouched down next to her. "Looks like Palmer got in the back, bypassed the security system like a pro. He hit the one guard in the kitchen, used a stunner to take him out quick and quiet. From the looks of the living area, the second one gave him more trouble. They went a round in there. Mira must have been up here. If she had the door closed and was working, she wouldn't have heard anything. Room's fully soundproofed."

"So he takes out the security, four experienced cops, waltzes right in, dismantles her bracelet, and waltzes out with her. We underestimated him, Feeney." And for that she would forever blame herself. "He's not what he was when I took him down before. He's studied up, he's learned, he's gotten himself into condition. He made good use of three years in a cage."

"She knows how his mind works." Feeney laid his hand on her shoulder. "Mira knows how to handle this kind of guy. She'll use that. She'll keep her cool and use it."

"No one knows how his mind works this time around. Thinking I did was part of the problem all along. I fucked up here, Feeney, and Mira's going to pay for it."

"You're wrong. The only fucking up you're doing is thinking that way now."

"I thought he might use Roarke as bait. Because if he's been studying me he knows that's where he could hit me the hardest." She made herself breathe slow as she got to her feet. "But he knows me better than I figured. He knows she matters to me."

"And he'll count on that messing you up. You gonna let it?"

"No." She breathed in again, exhaled. "No. I need McNab to shake something loose. What's their ETA?"

"Midday tomorrow. They had some transpo delays. The transmissions are full of blips, but I got that he's dug into some financials."

"Shoot whatever you've got to my home unit. I'll be working from there."

"We'll want to tap your palm-link."

"Yeah, he'll have figured that, but we'll do it anyway." She met Feeney's eyes. "We take the steps."

"We'll get her back, Dallas."

"Yeah, we will." She turned the sealed bracelet over in her hand. "If he hurts her, I'm taking him out." She lifted her gaze again. "Whatever line I have to cross, I take him out."

When she walked outside, Roarke was waiting. She hadn't argued when he'd come with her and could only be grateful that he was there to drive home so her mind could be free to think.

"Feeney's going to be sending me data," she began as she climbed into the car. "Financials. You'll be able to extrapolate faster. The sweepers will go through Mira's house, but he won't have left much, if anything. Anyway, it's not a question of IDing him. Peabody and McNab won't be back until midday tomorrow, so we'll be working with whatever they can send us while they're en route."

"I took a look at the alarms and security. It's a very good system. He used a sophisticated bypass unit to take it out without triggering the auto. It's not something your average citizen can access easily. I can help you trace the source."

"Doesn't matter at this point. Later we can deal with it. It's just another thread he left dangling, figuring I'd waste time pulling it and getting nowhere."

She rubbed at the headache behind her eyes. "I've got uniforms canvasing. One of the neighbors might have seen or heard something. It's useless, but it's routine and we might get lucky."

She closed her eyes, forced herself to think past the fear. "She's got until tomorrow, midnight. Dave wants some tradition and symbolism. He wants to welcome in the new year with me, and he needs her to get me there."

Her voice was too cool, Roarke thought. Too controlled. He'd seen the hint of panic in her eyes, and the grief. He let her hold in both as they arrived home, as she walked directly up to her office and called up all necessary files.

She added hard-copy data to the investigator's board she'd set up. And when she shifted Mira's photo from one area to the other, her fingers shook.

"Eve." He took her shoulders, turned her around. "Let it out."

"Can't. Don't talk to me."

"You can't work around it." He only tightened his grip when she tried to jerk away. "Let it out. Let it out," he said in a gentler tone. "I know what she means to you."

"God." She wrapped her arms around him, curling her

hands up over his shoulders as she pressed her face into his neck. "Oh, God. Hold on. Just for a minute, hold on."

Her body shook, one hard wave of shudders after another. She didn't weep, but her breath hitched as he held her close. "I can't think about what he might do to her. If I think about it, I'll lose it."

"Then remember she's strong, and she's smart. She'll know what she has to do."

"Yeah." Her 'link signaled incoming data. "That'll be the financials."

"I'll start on them." He eased her back. "He won't win this round."

"Damn right."

She worked until her eyes and mind went blurry, then fueled up with coffee and worked some more. At just after two A.M. Feeney shot her more data. It told her that he, Peabody, and McNab were all still on the job.

"Basically," Roarke said, "this is just confirming what we already have. The accounts, the transfers. You need to find more. You need to look from a different angle." He glanced up to see Eve all but swaying on her feet. "And you need to sleep."

She would have argued, but it would have wasted time. "We both do. Just a little while. We can share the sleep chair. I want to stay close to this unit."

The caffeine in her system couldn't fight off exhaustion. Moments after closing her eyes, she fell into sleep. Where nightmares chased her.

Images of Mira trapped in a cage mixed and melded with memories of herself as a child, locked in a room. Horror, pain, fear lived in both places. He would come—Palmer, her father—he would come and he would hurt her because he could. Because he enjoyed it. Because she couldn't stop him.

Until she killed him.

But even then he came back and did it all again in her dreams.

She moaned in sleep, curled into Roarke.

It was the smell of coffee and food that woke her. She sat up with a jerk, blinked blindly in the dark, and found herself alone in the chair. She stumbled into the kitchen and saw Roarke already taking food from the AutoChef.

"You need to eat."

"Yeah, okay." But she went for the coffee first. "I was thinking about what you said, looking at a different angle." She sat, because he nudged her into a chair, and shoveled in food because it was in front of her. "What if he bought or rented this place he's got before he got to New York? A year ago, two years ago?"

"It's possible. I still haven't found any payments."

"Has to be there. Somewhere." She heard the ring of her palm-link from the other room and was on her feet. "Stay in here, do what you can to trace."

Deliberately she moved behind her desk, sat, composed her face. "Dallas."

"Good morning, Lieutenant. I hope you slept well."

"Like a top, Dave." She curled a hand under the desk.

"Good. I want you rested up for our date tonight. You've got, oh, let's see, just over sixteen and a half hours to get here. I have every confidence in you."

"You could tell me where you are, we can start our date early."

He laughed, obviously delighted with her. "And spoil the fun? I don't think so. We're puzzle solvers, Dallas. You find me by midnight and Dr. Mira will remain perfectly safe. That's providing you come to see me alone. I'll know if you bring uninvited guests, as I have full security. Any gate-crashers, and the good doctor dies immediately and in great physical distress. I want to dance with you, Dallas. Just you. Understood?"

"It's always been you and me, Dave."

"Exactly. Come alone, by midnight, and we'll finish what we started three years ago."

"I don't know that she's still alive."

He only smiled. "You don't know that she's not." And broke transmission.

"Another public 'link," Roarke told her. "Port Authority."

"I need the location. If I'm not there by midnight, he'll kill her." She rose, paced. "He's got a place, one with full security. He's not bullshitting there. He'll have cameras, in and out. Sensors. He didn't have time to set all that up in a week, so either the place came equipped with them or he ordered them from prison courtesy of the chaplain."

"We can access tax records, blueprints, specs. It'll take time."

"Time's running out. Let's get started."

At two she received word that Peabody and McNab had landed, and she ordered them to bring the unit to her home office. He was close, she thought again, and none of them should waste time working downtown.

The minute they walked in, she began outlining her plan of attack. "McNab, set up over there. Start checking out any financials, transfers, transmissions, using the chaplain's name. Or a combo of his and Palmer's. Peabody, contact Whitney, request a canvas of all private garages in the suspect area. I want uniforms, every warm body we can find, hitting the public parking facilities with orders to confiscate and review all security tapes for the past week."

"All, Lieutenant?"

"Every last one."

She swung around and into Roarke's office. Using his auxiliary unit, she called up data, shot it to screen. "I've got the residences of Palmer's targets in blue," she told Roarke. "We run from mid to upper Manhattan, heaviest population on the East Side. We need to concentrate on private homes in this ten-block radius. Unless something jumps out at you, disregard anything that doesn't fit this profile."

She rolled her shoulders to relieve the tension, closed her eyes to clear her mind. "It'll have a basement. Probably two stories in addition to it. Fully soundproofed and most likely with its own vehicle storage area. I've got them looking at public storage, but I'm betting he has his own. He

wants me to find him, goddamn it, so it can't be that hard.
He wants me to work for it but not to fail. It's just personal
for him, and without me . . ."

She trailed off, whirled around. "He needs me. Jesus.
Check my name. Check deeds, mortgages, leases using my
name."

"There's your new angle, Lieutenant," Roarke murmured as he set to work. "Very good."

"Toss it on screen," she asked even as she moved to
stand behind him and watch. As her name popped up with
a list of liber and folio numbers she swore again. "How
the hell did he get all that property?"

"That's not his, it's yours."

"What do you mean mine? I don't own anything."

"Properties I've transferred into your name." Roarke
spoke absently as he continued the scan.

"Transferred? What the hell for?"

He skimmed a finger lightly over her wedding ring and
earned a punch in the shoulder. "You're welcome."

"Take it back. All of it."

"It's complicated. Taxes. Really, you're doing me a fa-
vor. No, there's nothing here that isn't yours. We'll try a
combination of names."

She wanted, badly, to seethe, but she didn't have time.

They found three listings for the name David Dallas in
Manhattan.

"Get the property descriptions."

"I'm working on it. It takes a moment to hack into city
hall."

Barely more than that for Roarke, Eve noted as the data
flashed on screen. "No, that's downtown. Sex club. Try the
next." She gripped the back of his chair, straining with
impatience. "That's just out of the target area, but possible.
Hold that and run the last. I'll be damned." She almost
whispered it. "He reverted to type after all. That's his parents' house. He bought their place."

"Two and a half years ago," Roarke confirmed. "Using
the name David Dallas. Your man was thinking ahead.

Very far ahead. We'll find accounts in that name, or an account that he had and closed.''

"Five blocks from here. The son of a bitch is five blocks from here." She leaned down, kissed the top of Roarke's head, and strode back into her office. "I've found it," she announced, then looked at her wrist unit. "We've got seven hours to figure out how to take him down."

She would go in alone. She insisted on it. She agreed to go in wired. Agreed to surveillance and backup at half-block intervals surrounding the house. For luck she pinned on the badge Peabody had given her, then waited with growing impatience as Feeney checked the transmitter.

"You're on," he told her. "Nothing I found on the video disc had equipment that can tag this pretty little bug. We've got a decoy so he'll think he's found one and deactivated it."

"Good thinking."

"You got to do it this way." He nodded at her. "I'd do the same. But you better understand I hear anything I don't like, I'm coming in. Roarke." He stepped back as Roarke came into the room. "I'll give you a minute here."

Roarke crossed to her, tapped a finger on her badge. "Funny, you don't look like Gary Cooper."

"Who?"

He smiled. "*High Noon*, darling Eve, though the clock's turned around on this one. We have a date in a couple of hours."

"I remember. I've got a present coming. I can do this."

"Yes." He kissed her, softly. "I know. Give my best to Mira."

"You bet. The team's moving into place now. I have to go."

"I'll see you soon."

He waited until she was gone, then walked outside himself and climbed casually into Feeney's unit. "I'll be riding with you."

Feeney scratched his chin. "Dallas won't like it."

"That's a pity. I spent the last few hours studying the

schematics for the security on the Palmer house. I can by-pass it, by remote.''

"Can you, now?" Feeney said mildly.

Roarke turned his head, gave Feeney a level look. "I shouldn't need more than twenty minutes clear to manage it.''

Feeney pursed his lips and started down the drive. "I'll see what we can do about that.''

She went in at ten. It was best, she'd decided, not to cut it too close to the deadline. The old brownstone was lovely, in perfect repair. The security cameras and sensors were discreetly worked into the trim so as not to detract from its dignity.

As she walked to the door she was certain Palmer was watching. And that he was pleased. She gave the overhead camera a brief glance, then bypassed the locks with her master.

She closed the door at her back, heard the locks snick automatically back into place. As they did, the foyer lights flashed on.

"Good evening, Dallas." Palmer's voice flowed out of the intercom. "I'm so pleased you could make it. I was just assuring Doctor Mira that you'd be here soon so we could begin our end-of-year celebration. She's fine, by the way. Now, if you'd just remove your weapon—''

"No." She said it casually as she moved forward. "I'm not stripping down for you, Dave, so you can take me out as I come down the stairs. Let's not insult each other.''

He laughed. "Well, I suppose you're right. Keep it. Take it out. Engage it. It's fine. Just remember, Doctor Mira's fate is in your hands. Come join us, Lieutenant. Let's party.''

She'd been in the house before, when she interviewed his parents. Even if the basic setup hadn't come back to her, she'd taken time to study the blueprints. Still, she didn't move too quickly, but scanned cautiously for booby traps on the way through the house.

She turned at the kitchen, opened the basement door. The sound of cheering blasted up at her. The lights were on bright. She could see streamers, balloons, festive decorations.

She took her weapon out and started down.

He had champagne chilling in a bucket, pretty canapés spread on silver trays on a table draped with a colorful cloth.

And he had Mira in a cage.

"Lieutenant Dallas." Mira said it calmly, though her mind was screaming. She'd been careful to call Eve by her title, to keep their relationship professional, distant.

"Doctor." Palmer clucked his tongue. "I told you I'd do the talking. Lieutenant, you see this control I'm holding. Just so we understand each other right away, if I press this button, a very strong current will pass through the metal of the doctor's temporary home. She'll be dead in seconds. Even with your weapon on full, I'll have time to engage it. Actually, my nervous system will react in such a way to the shock that my finger will twitch involuntarily, and the doctor, shall we say, is toasted."

"Okay, Dave, but I intend to verify that Doctor Mira is unharmed. Are you hurt, Doctor?"

"No." And she'd managed so far to hold back hysteria. "He hasn't hurt me. And I don't think he will. You won't hurt me, will you, David? You know I want to help you. I understand how difficult all this has been for you, not having anyone who appreciates what you've been working to achieve."

"She's really good, isn't she?" he said to Eve. "So soothing. Since I don't want to show her any disrespect— you'll note I didn't remove her clothing for our little experiment—maybe you should tell her to shut the fuck up. Would you mind, Dallas?"

"Dave and I need to handle this, Dr. Mira." Eve moved closer. "Don't we, Dave? It's you and me."

"I've waited for this for so long. You can see I've gone to quite a bit of trouble." He gestured with his free hand. "Maybe you'd like a drink, an hors d'oeuvre. We have a celebration going on. The end of the old, the birth of the new. Oh, and before I jam that wire you're wearing, tell

the backup team that if anyone attempts entry, you both
die.''

"I'm sure they heard you. And they already have orders
to hold back. You said to come alone," she reminded him.
"So I did. I always played it straight with you."

"That's right. We learned to trust each other."

"Why stop now? I've got a deal for you, Dave. A trade.
Me for Mira. You let her out of there, you let her go, and
I'll get in. You'll have what you want."

"Eve, don't—" Mira's composure started to slip.

"This is between me and Dave." She kept her eye on
him, level and cool. "That's what you want, isn't it? To
put me in a cage, the way I put you in one. You've been
thinking about it for three years. You've been planning it,
working for it, arranging it step by step. And you did a
damn good job this time around. Let her go, Dave. She was
just bait, you got me here by using her. Let her go and I'll
put down my weapon. I'll get in, and you'll have the kind
of subject you've always wanted."

She took another step toward him, watching his eyes
now, watching them consider. Desire. "She's a shrink, and
she's not in the kind of condition I'm in—mental or physical. She sits at a desk and pokes into other people's minds.
You start on her, she'll go down fast, give you no satisfaction. Think how long I'll last. Not just hours, days. Maybe
weeks if you can hold the outside team off that long. You
know it's going to end here, for both of us."

"Yes, I'm prepared for that."

"But this way, you can get your payback and finish your
work. Two for one. But you have to let her out."

Music crashed out of the entertainment unit. On screen
the revelers in Times Square swarmed like feverish ants.

"Put down the weapon now."

"Tell me it's a deal." She held her breath, lifted her
weapon, aimed it at the center of his body. "Tell me it's a
deal or I take you down. She goes, but I live. And you lose
all around. Take the deal, Dave. You'll never get a better
one."

"I'll take the deal." All but quivering with excitement,

he rubbed a hand over his mouth. "Put the weapon down. Put it down and move away from it."

"Bring the cage down first. Bring it down to the floor so I know you mean it."

"I can still kill her." But he reached out to the console, touched a switch. The cage began to sway and lower.

"I know it. You've got the power here. I've just got a job. I'm sworn to protect her. Unlock the cage."

"Put the weapon down!" He shouted it out now, raising his voice over the music and cheers. "You said you'd put it down, now do it!"

"Okay. We've got a deal." Sweat slid down her back as she bent to lay the weapon on the floor. "You don't kill for the hell of it. It's for science. Unlock the cage and let her go." Eve lifted her hands, palms out.

On a bright laugh, he grabbed up a stunner, jabbed the air with it. "Just in case. You stay where you are, Dallas."

Her heart began to beat again when he put the control down, hit the button to release the locks. "Sorry you have to leave the party, Doctor Mira. But I promised this dance to the lieutenant."

"I need to help her out." Eve crouched to take Mira's hand. "Her muscles are stiff. She wouldn't have lasted for you, Dave." She gave Mira's hand one hard squeeze.

"Get in, get in now."

"As soon as she's clear." Eve remained crouched, pushed Mira aside. As she used her body as a shield, she had time to register a movement on the stairs, then her clinch piece was in her hand.

"I lied, Dave." She watched his eyes go round with shock, saw him grab for the control, lower the stunner. The crowd cheered wildly as her blast took him full in the chest.

His body jerked, a quick and obscene dance. He was right, she noted, about the finger twitch. It depressed convulsively on the control even as he fell onto the cage.

Sparks showered from it, from his quaking body as she dragged Mira clear and curled herself over her.

"Your jacket's caught fire, Lieutenant." With admirable

calm, Roarke bent over and patted out the spark that burned the leather at her shoulder.

"What the hell are you doing here?"

"Just picking up my wife for our date." He reached down gently and helped Mira to her feet. "He's gone," Roarke murmured, and brushed tears from her cheeks.

"I couldn't reach him. I tried, for hours after I woke up in that . . . in that thing. But I couldn't reach him." Mira turned to Eve. "You could, in the only way that was left. I was afraid you'd—" She broke off, shook her head. "I was afraid you'd come, and afraid you wouldn't. I should have trusted you to do what had to be done."

When she caught Eve in a hard embrace, pressed her cheek against hers, Eve held on, just held on, then eased away, awkwardly patting Mira's back. "It was a team effort—including this civilian this time around. Go spend New Year's with your family. We'll worry about the routine later."

"Thank you for my life." She kissed Eve's cheek, then turned and kissed Roarke's. And didn't begin to weep again until she was upstairs.

"Well, Lieutenant, it's a very fitting end."

She followed Roarke's gaze, studied Palmer, and felt nothing but quiet relief. "To the man or the year?"

"To both." He stepped to the champagne, sniffing it as he drew it from the bucket. "Your team's on the way in. But I think we could take time for a toast."

"Not here. Not with that." She took the bottle, dumped it back into the bucket. On impulse, she took the badge off her shirt, pinned it on his. "Routine can wait. I want to collect on my present."

"Where do you want to go?"

"Just home." She slid an arm around his waist, moving toward the stairs as cops started down. "Just home, with you." She heard the crowd erupt with another cheer. "Happy New Year."

"Not quite yet. But it will be."